MANHATTAN SHOOTING

Written by

Joe McNeil

Copyright © 2023 Joe McNeil.

All rights reserved. No part of this book may be reproduced, stored, or transmitted by any means—whether auditory, graphic, mechanical, or electronic—without written permission of both publisher and author, except in the case of brief excerpts used in critical articles and reviews. Unauthorized reproduction of any part of this work is illegal and is punishable by law.

This is a work of fiction. Names, characters, places and incidents either are the product of the author's imagination or are used fictitiously, and any resemblance to any actual persons, living or dead, events, or locales is entirely coincidental.

ISBN: 979-8-89031-498-7 (sc)
ISBN: 979-8-89031-499-4 (hc)
ISBN: 979-8-89031-500-7 (e)

Library of Congress Control Number: 2014903849

Because of the dynamic nature of the Internet, any web addresses or links contained in this book may have changed since publication and may no longer be valid. The views expressed in this work are solely those of the author and do not necessarily reflect the views of the publisher, and the publisher hereby disclaims any responsibility for them.

One Galleria Blvd., Suite 1900, Metairie, LA 70001
(504) 702-6708
1-888-421-2397

CONTENTS

Chapter 1 The Shooting 1
Chapter 2 New York's Finest 5
Chapter 3 Meeting the Press 11
Chapter 4 Meeting with Clarkston 15
Chapter 5 Front-Page News 21
Chapter 6 Seclusion 27
Chapter 7 The Siege 35
Chapter 8 Cover Up 43
Chapter 9 Road Trip 47
Chapter 10 Recon Begins 53
Chapter 11 The Trap 58
Chapter 12 Obtaining The List 62
Chapter 13 A New Member 66
Chapter 14 Selective Hunting 72
Chapter 15 Warren Connection 77
Chapter 16 Evading the Net 80
Chapter 17 The 911 Assist 90
Chapter 18 Hunt Resumed 94

Chapter 19	Helicopter Support	104
Chapter 20	The Bug	110
Chapter 21	Turning the Table	121
Chapter 22	Cat and Mouse	128
Chapter 23	Turning the Tide	136
Chapter 24	Standing Down	141
Chapter 25	Uninvited Guest	149
Chapter 26	Arriving at D.C.	171

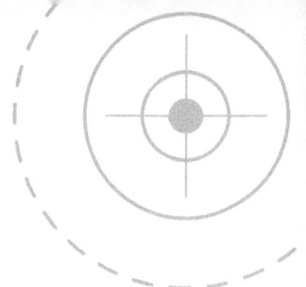

CHAPTER 1

THE SHOOTING

Without thinking I headed for the window, compelled to find out where the sound of the shots had originated. I, like many others in my building, stood in front of our windows scanning the area for the source of the gunfire. I didn't give a second thought about my safety; curiosity had its deadly grip on my life and thrust me closer to the unopened window. I never even had time to flinch when the first bullet zinged by my head right through the glass. I stood there; mouth agape and my eyes were still searching for the shooter. When my brain forced me to my knees in an attempt to save my life, my eyes were still trying to find the shooter. *How crazy was that I thought as I lay there on the hardwood floor of my Upper Manhattan apartment?*

I lay there motionless for several minutes, the sound of additional shots and other glass breaking sang through the walls of my apartment. Finally I mustered the strength to pull myself away from the window. *Curiosity still gripping at my mind I found myself being led to slaughter again, this time it was behind the louvered window of my bedroom, I must be mad.* I peered through the bottom of the window when finally I saw the muzzle flash from a rifle. Across the street, about the 11th floor, that is when I remembered my binoculars. As quickly as I could I ran to the hall closet, digging through the years of failed hobbies, I finally found them. I hurried back across the apartment, like a kid missing cartoons, I trained my binoculars onto the 11th floor where I had seen the flash. After a few minor adjustments to the focus of the binoculars I saw him. I expected some enraged homeless person to be causing all this chaos, instead he was well dressed, mid-thirties, business type. I stared in disbelief as I watched him empty his rifle into our apartment building, one shot after another, seldom taking the time needed to aim. He pulled his empty clip and rammed another in its place.

What could be so wrong that would cause someone like him to go so crazy? I decided to try and get a picture of the shooter, my camera was not set up with a great zoom lens but I felt like I had to do something. I rushed back across the apartment to my hall closet; the keeper of failed hobbies, and found my camera bag. A Nikon 35MM with film from the 90's, I hoped the pictures would turn out.

I sat up my camera on the base of the bedroom window and stuck the lens through the louver. I snapped off a few quick pictures not thinking about the shooter reacting to the flash of my camera strobe. Just as I was adjusting the lens for a closer shot I saw the barrel of his rifle pointed directly at my window. I rolled to the side, clinging to my camera, as I did, three bullets ripped through my bedroom window sending my window blinds crashing onto my bed.

Afraid that he would come across the street looking for me I panicked and headed for the elevator. As I reached for the lobby button, I envisioned the elevator door opening into the lobby and the shooter standing in front of the elevator and filling my body with holes. Instead of pressing the down button, I pressed the button-marked roof.

The elevator doors opened onto the roof and I climbed out. At the end of a short hallway was a big steel door, people in the building come up here from time to time in the summer to work on their tans. I opened the door and wedged a piece of rebar steel into the doorframe to keep the door from locking me out. I moved across the rooftop in a crouched position so as not to be seen by the shooter. When I reached the edge of the building I began looking through the lens of my camera for the shooter's apartment room. I found him; his rifle was still trained on my apartment window. I took my strobe off the camera and again tried to zoom in on the shooter. As I began snapping shots I watched as the shooter slump over across the back of the chair he was using for a gun rest. Seconds later two men in black suits were standing next to the body, I assumed they were detectives, instinctively I snapped a couple of pictures for my scrap book. I even thought that perhaps the newspaper or a magazine might purchase one or two of them.

I sat there daydreaming about the opportunity of getting rich off of these pictures when I noticed the two men were removing the body of the shooter. I quickly snapped a couple additional pictures and decided to go down and turn on the news to see if they were talking about the shooting. Even in New York this type of shooting might be news worthy. When I got back to my apartment I went into my bedroom to survey the damage done by the shooter. I glanced out of my window and there was a man in the shooter's room scanning our apartment building with some hi-tech binoculars. They looked like something from a science fiction futuristic spy movie. I watched, as he appeared to be scanning each apartment that received any fire. I decided it wouldn't hurt to take a couple pictures of this joker. As I snapped the first picture the film began to rewind. I had taken my last picture on this roll. I hurried over to my camera bag and reloaded the film; I used the new film canister for the old film and slipped it into my pocket.

Returning to the window to continue my picture history the man with the space-age binoculars had left. I decided to try and take a few pictures of the inside of the apartment. I re-focused into the room and began to snap. I had taken several pictures and then backed away from my window and took a few additional snaps of my bedroom window and the damage to the walls of my apartment. It wasn't until then that I noticed one of the bullets had struck my DVD player. I took a couple additional shots of my room and moved to the living room to repeat the process.

Finally I remembered the reason for returning to the apartment was to watch the news on TV. I turned the TV on and changed the channel to the local news. The screen was all a buzz about the shooter. The news lady said the police were still looking for the shooter. I laughed to myself; for once I was more informed than the news. I knew the police had already found and shot the shooter. I moved to my window again and peered down towards the street. I was expecting an ambulance, S.W.A.T. and several police cars to be parked on the street.

To my amazement there were only two police cars, no ambulance, no S.W.A.T. team and no shooter. This couldn't be right, I saw the shooter slump in his chair, and I know the police shot him. As I sat there listening to the news I began to wonder if maybe the pictures I had taken could really be worth some money now since the news people don't seem to know what happen.

I grabbed my camera and hurried off for the elevator. When I reached the lobby several people from my building were being interviewed by the police officers. I pushed by the crowd and hurried down to the corner to the one-hour photo store.

I asked the girl behind the desk if she could put a rush on my film. In typical New York fashion she replied, "Fill out the form on the front of the envelope, place your film in the envelope, if you want one-hour development check the box which indicates one-hour, when you have completed all the information on the form and returned the form to me I will time stamp the envelope." She continued, "At that point I will drop everything else there is to do in the high paying job and rush this film through the development process, standing over the developer every step of the way making sure your precious film is expedited!"

Completing each line of the form and placing the film in the envelope I handed the film to her for time stamping. She snatched the envelope from my hand and dropped it into a basket with several other envelopes, glanced up at me and said, "The film will be ready in the morning, have a nice day!"

New York, it is quite a large step from Texas. I started to get angry and snap back at her, instead I just said thank you and headed for the door.

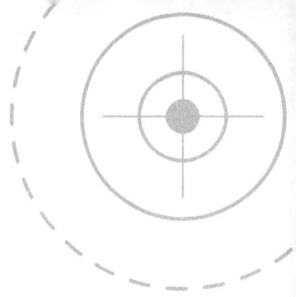

CHAPTER 2

NEW YORK'S FINEST

A rriving back at my apartment building, a police officer stopped me at the door and asked, "Did you see anything that took place here?"

"If you mean the shooting," I replied, "I saw the whole thing, I even got pictures."

I even got pictures was the wrong thing to say to a young street beat cop in New York. His demeanor went from I'm bored-out-of-my-gourd attitude to an instant I'm going to make detective for this one. He reached for my camera and almost yanked it from around my neck. I was going to explain to him that the film he really wanted was getting developed, or at least should be developed by morning; instead I decided I would look at the pictures in the morning and take the police a couple that the newspapers didn't buy. The overly zealous officer said, "Your name and address."

Oddly enough this struck me funny, since this apartment building was my address. I began to laugh aloud. Not at all amused by my outbreak the officer retorted, "What is so funny about your name and address?"

I replied, "Sorry officer Carmichael is it, I assumed because you were standing inside my apartment building you knew what my address was. It just struck me funny that you would ask."

He responded, "Carmichael is correct, you're not from New York are you. Texas I bet."

"Yes, that is amazing, I didn't realize I still had an accent." "Who cares," he snapped. "I still need your name and address."

I replied, "Chris Moore, apartment 1218, Moore Towers and no I don't own the building."

"Did I ask if you owned the building," he snapped? "Is Chris Moore your whole name?"

"No, my whole name is Joseph Christopher Moore."

"Why didn't you say that from the start?"

"I didn't realize you needed my whole name," I insisted.

Feeling put out at the New York attitude, I thought, come to Texas and try that crap. Of course thinking back, I am sure nothing different would have transpired in Texas. The officer snapped me out of my daydream by asking, "Would you accompany me to headquarters?"

I asked, "Could I get freshened up first?"

"No," replied the officer, "I am not really asking you to come; I am telling you to come to my headquarters."

Rather than argue with this flatfoot, I decided to wait until I could speak with a detective, perhaps his attitude will be less abrasive. "Since you asked me so nicely," I replied, "I will be happy to come down to your headquarters."

As we exited the building I went around to the passenger side of his squad car and waited for him to let me in. Instead of reaching across to let me in, he lowered the window and said, "Backseat."

"Backseat, if I ride in the back seat someone might see me and think I am under arrest," I complained.

He answered, "If you don't get in the back seat, your friends won't have to think you are under arrest, you will be!"

"The backseat is fine with me," I replied as I opened the back door.

There was no conversation on our way to police headquarters. I simply passed the time revisiting the events that had just transpired and trying to decide how much information to divulge to the police. I knew they weren't in any position to pay me for the pictures I had taken.

Pulling down into the parking garage of the 12th Precinct and coming to a halt in a parking spot, I tried to exit the car by lifting the door lever. Nothing happened. I looked into the front seat of the car and said, "I can't get the door to open."

Without comment, Carmichael reached to the passenger seat and grabbed his hat then opened the back door on his side of the car. I slid across the seat and accompanied him to the elevator. When the doors of the elevator shut I asked, "What are we going to do here?"

Officer Carmichael said, "We will ask you questions and you will answer them."

"That's nice, I didn't think we were going to have lunch."

Officer Carmichael smirked and replied, "Lunch can be arranged, just pop off one more time."

As we stepped out of the elevator on the third floor, it was a totally different scene than I had expected. There were old metal desks back to back, no dividing walls in one large room. The room looked more like a pressroom from a 50's movie than an office full of detectives.

A voice shouted from across the room and said, "Carmichael why isn't your girlfriend wearing bracelets?"

Carmichael replied, "Not my girlfriend, he witnessed the shooting at Moore Towers."

A momentary hush came over the room, when a big-bellied detective shuffled his way in our direction. His suit looked like he had been sleeping on a park bench for several days. As he approached I notice a scar on his cheek just below his bifocals, I tried not to stare at him. His face looked like he had been an unsuccessful sparring partner for some heavy weight champ to pound on. What hair remained on his head was gray and un-kept.

The detective and Officer Carmichael stood off to the side and had a lengthy discussion. At some point during this discussion my camera changed hands from Officer Carmichael to this jug-head detective. Finally, their conversation was over and the detective pointed his big finger directly at me and motioned for me to take a seat in the chair beside his desk.

As I approached his desk I noticed his name was Detective Lensky, I thought to myself, *"Great this big lug is going to try and intimidate me into confessing to all the unsolved murders in New York."*

As I reached the chair he exclaimed, "Name and address?"

What is this with the New York police force; don't they know how to have a simple greeting without this entire tuff guy attitude? "Joseph Christopher Moore, apartment 1218, Moore Towers," I complied.

"Mr. Moore, seems you were an eyewitness to the shootings into your apartment building."

"Yes, I even took pictures of the shooter."

"Not so fast, Mr. Moore, I have to type out a statement for you to sign and even though you talk like your tongue was ran over by a steam roller I still don't type that fast."

Could be he detects a bit of a Texas accent. At least I can type as fast as I can think; maybe he can too! I hate this smug New York attitude, if you're not born and raised in New York they assume you are less intelligent and have half the common sense it takes to push a broom.

During the middle of typing out my statement, Detective Lensky stops typing and picks up the phone. He asks someone to come by and pick up my camera and have the film developed. It was at that point that I should have told him about the other roll of film, but if I did, they would only go and pick it up and I never would make any money off of it. So I decided to not include the changing of film into my statement.

After what seemed hours, the statement was typed up, as I scanned the contents of the statement for accuracy, Detective Lensky grew impatient waiting on me to proof the statement. He said, "Are you going to take the rest of my day reading what you said?"

I replied, "I have found several typos but the rest of the report is correct."

I picked up a pen and signed the report. As I completed my signature Lensky snatched the statement from my hand and placed it into a folder that was labeled, Moore Towers.

Detective Lensky grabbed the phone and growled at the person on the other end about what was taking so long to get those pictures developed. I thought, *"Fill out the form on the front of the envelope, place your film in the envelope, if you want one-hour development check the box which indicates one-hour, when you have completed all the information on the form and returned the form to me I will time stamp the envelope. At that point I will drop everything else there is to do in the high paying job and rush this film through the development process, standing over the developer every step of the way making sure your precious film is expedited!"* Lensky interrupted my wise guy thinking by slamming his phone onto the receiver. I looked up expecting him to tell me it wasn't going to be until tomorrow when the film gets developed. Instead he said, "The developer tells me there are only shots of the apartment building across from your apartment on the film and there is no shooter. The rest of the pictures are the inside of an apartment which was shot up by the shooter, I assume it is your apartment."

I replied, "Oh yea, I thought I would need a photo history for my insurance."

Detective Lensky leaned out over his desk towards me and said; "You know it is a crime to make a false report to the police?"

I explained, "I did see the shooter and can give a fairly accurate description of him and the two officers that shot him."

Detective Lensky threw back his chair, stood up in front of me; his eyes looked as though he was going to rip my head from my shoulders. I flinched in anticipation of brute force and he said, "Your statement didn't say a thing about two officers shooting the shooter nor did you mention the shooter being shot and if the police had shot this nut we wouldn't be having this conversation."

Before I could explain about the other roll of film he yelled, "Get the hell out of my sight before I book you for obstruction and false reporting."

Without another word I jumped out of my chair and headed for the door. Lensky shouted after me, "The next time you are sitting in my chair it will be with bracelets on your wrist; You Punk!"

I almost turned back and told him about the second roll of film, but somehow it didn't seem fair to let him get any glory after he humiliated me in front of all those detectives. Staying my coarse through the door and down towards the elevator, I began to smile inside. I knew that when the newspapers received my pictures that Detective Lensky would have to eat those words. This gave me a feeling of great satisfaction.

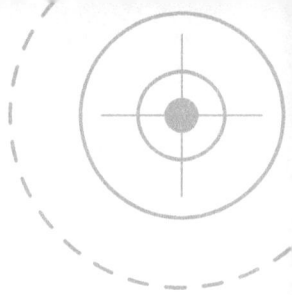

CHAPTER 3

MEETING THE PRESS

In the lobby of the police building I remembered my camera, I started to go back up and get it, but I didn't want to face Detective Lensky again. I walked out of the police station and hailed a cab.

The cabby inquired, "Where to, Mister?" I answered, "Texas."

The cabby wheeled his head around towards me, daggers already shooting from his eyes and said, "Look Mac, there are already enough comedians in this city and further more my wife is funnier than you are . . . and she's a bore, now where would you like to be taken."

I replied, "Take me to Moore Towers."

The cabby grabbed the meter arm and peeled away from the curb. As we neared the apartments I told him to stop at the photo shop. I paid him and before I could utter keep the change he sped off, in a typical New York fashion.

I knew there was an outside chance that my film could possibly be ready. I entered the store and went to the counter and asked if the pictures for Chris Moore were ready. The man behind the counter turned to the baskets full of envelopes marked rush and said, "What's your name buddy?"

"Moore, Chris Moore."

The guy behind the counter looked up and smiled, "Looks like you are in luck, your film is right here. That will be sixteen ninety five, cash or charge?"

"Sixteen ninety five, I hope there are some good pictures on this roll."

After paying for the pictures I moved towards the door to catch the light coming through the window to view the pictures. The first few pictures were of the lady that caused me to decide to get into photography as a hobby in the first place. I thought back to the time I spent with her and remember that she dumped me for an old boyfriend of hers shortly after these pictures were taken. Oh well . . . the rest of the pictures on the roll were great. They looked like a professional had taken them. I turned back to the man behind the counter and asked, "Can you enlarge a couple of these pictures for me?"

He said, "I can enlarge the entire roll if that is what you want, but it is going to set you back more than sixteen ninety five."

I started to hand him the pictures I wanted enlarged and he said, "Look buddy, in this business we give you the pictures, you give us the negatives."

He pulled the negatives from my envelope and marked the two pictures I wanted enlarged. He said, "These will be ready in about a week."

The two pictures I was having enlarged were a clear shot of the shooter and a clear shot of the two detectives that shot him. I was going to stick these pictures in Detective Lensky's face. I thanked the man at the photo shop and headed for the door.

Outside I hailed another cab. When the cab pulled to the curb he said, "Where to Joe?"

I replied, "Take me to the New York Times building."

As we were pulling away from the curb the cabby with his eyes in the rearview asked, "Are those two men in the suits with you?"

MEETING THE PRESS

I looked back to see two men slowing from their sprint to the cab and replied, "Nope, I have never seen them before in my life."

The trip to the Times was quick. It was a large tower on the edge of the Big Apple. After paying the cab driver I walked into the front door of the Times building. I told the receptionist that I had some pictures that might be of interest to one of their reporters. She said, "First things first, please sign our sign in log."

Upon complying with this request she asked, "Are you freelance or employed by a magazine?"

I thought for a moment, and then replied, "Freelance."

The receptionist smirked and said, "Perhaps you would be better severed trying somewhere else to peddle your pictures."

I replied with elevated tone, "If you don't want pictures of the shooter at Moore Towers and pictures of the men that shot him it is fine with me." I turned and started moving towards the front doors.

She called after me, "Just a minute, let me call the editor."

I stopped and went back to stand in front of her reception desk. When she hung up the phone she said, "Please make yourself at home. Can I bring you anything?"

I headed towards the plush chairs in the middle of the lobby and replied, "A Pepsi would be nice."

About the time I reached the chair a young man showed up with a twenty ounce Pepsi and a glass full of ice. I was impressed. I had just finished pouring the Pepsi into the glass and taking a sip or two when I noticed an elderly gentleman at the receptionist desk. The receptionist pointed in my direction and he immediately headed directly for me.

The man introduced himself to me by saying, "Mr. Moore, please don't get up. I am John Clarkston, editor of The Times and I am very interested in viewing your pictures."

"Before we look at the pictures, I would like to know what kind of money we are talking."

Mr. Clarkston replied, "If you have pictures of the shooter and a cover up, we are talking whatever amount our lawyers will allow us to pay you, that is of course if you sign a letter of exclusivity with us."

"Ballpark figures, what are we talking," I enquired?

Mr. Clarkston smiled and said, "Minimum five figures, maximum six."

I replied, "Six is a number I can work with."

Mr. Clarkston said, "Done, if the pictures are legitimate. Now let's see the pictures."

I pulled the pictures from the envelope and handed them to the editor. He scanned through them hastily until he came to the picture of the two men picking up the shooter's body. His face paled and he said, "Mr. Moore, if you don't mind let's take these pictures upstairs where we can be a little more comfortable."

"I don't mind at all, as long as we are still talking six figures."

Mr. Clarkston replied, "I am not sure we will be able to run the entire story, the first thing we will have to do is find out who these two men are and who they are working for."

"What about my money? Mr. Clarkston, will I still get my money?"

Mr. Clarkston said, "Call me John, and of course you will get your money. I am just not sure how much of your story we can print."

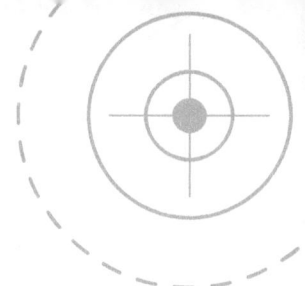

CHAPTER 4

MEETING WITH CLARKSTON

As we exited the elevator, the floor was as plush as the finest hotel in the city. I looked up and chandeliers were used to light the halls, real crystal not that imitation stuff. When we approached the double doors of Mr. Clarkston's office he looked towards me and asked, "Chris can I get you something a little stronger to drink?"

Caught up in the moment I replied, "No thanks John, this is fine." *First name basis with someone as important as this and all because I took a few pictures, cool!*

John continued, "Chris have a seat, I will call our legal team and a few of my ace reporters to get to work on your money and your story. Have you told anyone else at all about the two men that shot the shooter?"

I replied, "Well, I did mention to the police that I took pictures of the shooter, but when they developed the second roll of film there was only pictures of my apartment and the shooter's apartment on it. I also told them about the two cops that shot the shooter."

John said, "Ok Chris, this is getting messy. Let's start with the second roll of film. Where is the film now?"

"When I re-entered my apartment building after dropping the first roll off to get it developed, the second roll of film was in my camera. When I told Officer Carmichael that I had pictures of the shooter he snatched my camera and asked me to come down town with him. At the 12th Precinct he handed my camera to detective Lensky. Lensky had someone come get my camera and develop the film."

John started to ask more questions when his phone rang. John answered and said, "Send them in." After a brief pause, he said, "Yes, all of them."

Looking over at me as he was placing the phone on his receiver he said, "Your money, the lawyers and contracts are on their way in. A couple of reporters will be with them, we will not start working on your story until you sign the contract."

"When do I get to find out how much money we are talking"?

John looked at me with disappointment in his eyes and said, "Chris, you are going to be paid around two hundred and fifty thousand dollars if the story and your pictures check out. Is the money the only reason you came up here today?"

I lowered my head, feeling a little guilty about the answer I was going to give and said, "Yes, what else would I have come for?"

John forced a smile onto his face and said, "If you were a report and someone told you that they had the story of the year, an eyewitness of a shooting and a cover up all rolled into one neat package with photos, Pulitzer's Prize would be the first thing you thought of over money."

When the lawyers and the reporters entered Mr. Clarkston's office and the introductions were out of the way, the atmosphere became chaotic. Questions were coming at me from all directions. I looked over at John and asked, "Is there some way we can be a little more organized? I am answering the same questions over and over."

Mr. Clarkston replied, "Gentlemen, wouldn't it be better if we let Chris give you a recap of the day's events, then if you have any questions we will work it as though we were in a press conference. I want to get these pictures enlarged and clean up the background."

I replied, "I gave the negatives to the photo shop on the corner by my apartment to have a few of the pictures enlarged."

MEETING WITH CLARKSTON

Mr. Clarkston pressed a button on his desk and said, "Turner I need you to go to the corner of Bellows and Grace in Manhattan and pick up any pictures and the negatives for a Mr. Chris Moore."

"Saddler, get one of your youngsters and send them to the 12th Precinct and have Mr. Moore's camera and film picked up. If there is any problems have your boy start the paperwork to get a court order," Mr. Clarkston instructed.

Mr. Clarkston turned to me and asked, "Start from the beginning of the shooting and take everyone in the room through the events of the day."

I started telling of the events of the day and when I completed the story, one of the reporters named Harris asked, "Are you willing to go into hiding?"

"Hiding, I laughed, are you planning on siding with Detective Lensky and accuse me of every unsolved crime in New York?"

Harris replied, "No, but it looks as though the shooter worked for a secret organization and either went over the top and just started randomly shooting or the men you assumed shot the shooter only staged the shooting to get their man out of the building in case anyone was watching."

"So you think this is some sort of cloak-and-dagger thing?"

"I'm not sure, but if the shooter actually hit his intended victim then continued firing to cover the situation we will soon find out. We are doing a background check on everybody in your building from the 11th floor to the roof," Harris replied.

Mr. Clarkston interrupted by saying, "First let's get the lawyers working on the contract for Mr. Moore."

The next few questions were follow-ups by the lawyers to ensure that I was going to sign a letter of exclusivity. Then the biggest question of all was posed; the lawyers looked at me and asked, "Have you ever gone by another name or an alias?"

MANHATTAN SHOOTING

This question hit me hard. *At one time I worked for a group inside the United States that disrupted narcotic chains. Some of these chains were run by other organizations within the United States that didn't exactly appreciate our methods of correcting problems. I was given an opportunity to semi-retire from that line of work and was relocated to New York. I assumed at the time that it was some form of punishment to send a Texan to New York to hide out. For several years, I stuck out like a sore thumb. That line of work allowed me to live like a jetsetter except when I was undercover or on an assignment. During the 80's and early 90's I was always on assignment. The work dropped off during the Clinton administration and I was offered an opportunity to pursue a carrier with some form of future.*

"Mr. Moore, Mr. Moore, can you answer the question," demanded one of the lawyers?

"Yes, I have used an alias, when I was employed by the Government."

"Mr. Moore, for what reasons would you use your alias?"

"To keep people from knowing who I was, why else would you use an alias?"

"Are you willing to allow us to publish your alias in the story or reveal your name as the source of the story?"

"Absolutely not, I must remain anonymous for reasons I choose not to discuss with this paper or anybody else for that matter."

"Have you ever been arrested or convicted of any crimes?"

"No, never convicted of any crimes. What does this have to do with the story?"

"If your story comes into dispute and they find out that you are some sort of criminal element it could damage the reputation of the newspaper for harboring you from the police."

"What are they talking about here John? Harboring me from the police, they are acting like the police will be after me when this story gets out. All I want is to get my money and go back to my apartment call my insurance company and get my room fixed."

Mr. Clarkston replied, "Chris it is not going to be that cut and dry, you will be under contract to the newspaper until the story is printed and all the follow ups are exhausted. Did you think we were going to turn over a quarter of a million dollars and not have any strings attached?"

"Well yes, yes I did. When I came into the newspaper this afternoon I was planning on making from a few hundred to a couple thousand dollars for some pictures. I wasn't looking to give you the story of the year or become a prisoner of the newspaper."

"If you would settle for five thousand dollars right now for the film, the story and signing a gag ordered contract you can be on your way. When the police pick you up for questioning however we cannot assist you by invoking the first amendment rights."

"What makes you think the police will pick me up?"

"When the pictures of the shooter slumped in the chair run in the follow up story to the shooting and the two men that carried him out of the building make front page news; you are the police's only witness. I am sure they will pick you up."

"So if I stay here I will receive a quarter of a million dollars and be placed in hiding from the police by the newspaper?"

"Yes, we will pay you when the stories run, if you abide by the terms of the contract, we will hide you from the police and the men, yet identified in the picture."

"OK, OK, I see the advantages to working with the paper, I'll sign the contract. Now let's finish the questioning, I am getting hungry."

John reached for his phone on the desk and instructed his secretary to bring in several menus from local restaurants. She entered the room; scanning the room for faces she did not recognize and trained her eyes on me. John took the menus from her hand and handed them to me saying, "Go ahead, and name your poison."

I replied, "Poison? That's really not my choice of wording, how about Chinese?"

"Chinese it is," John smiled. "Now let's get the orders taken and we will have someone sent out to pick up the food."

John again reached for the phone; this time asked, "Where are we with getting the background information I requested, the pictures from the police and the negatives from the photo shop?"

One of the lawyers, Saddler, I believe was his name asked, "Did you know the shooter or any of the men in these pictures?"

"I don't believe so; I didn't take that much time to study the pictures. I didn't recognize any of them at a glance."

"What about the man with the binoculars, what role did he have in this story?"

"I took a picture of some guy in the shooter's room with high-tech binoculars scanning my apartment building. I don't know who the man was, put I did know he was in the shooter's room so I took a picture of him. I assumed he was a cop."

Several additional questions were asked and answered. The phone rang to announce the food had arrived. We all took a break to eat. While the meal of being consumed, John remained on the phone. I could not hear all that was being said but from the tone of his voice I could tell he was not pleased. It was nearing the deadline for the front-page to be printed and confirmation of anyone being shot had not been obtained from the police or other outside sources of the newspaper.

After the meal, the questioning continued until the late night news came on with a blurb about the shooting at my apartment building. The story stated that in upper Manhattan today, an unknown shooter fired countless times into the Moore Building. Police have no one in custody and no leads as to the identity of the shooter. After the news story was over John announced we should break for the night. He had one of his reporters take me to a nearby hotel and check me into a suite used by the Times for VIPs.

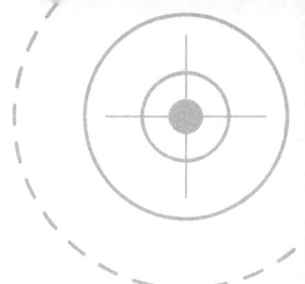

CHAPTER 5

FRONT-PAGE NEWS

The following morning around eight o'clock a knock at the door aroused me from my slumber. When I got to the door there was no one outside only three local newspapers, one of which was the New York Times. I picked up the three papers and chose to save the Times for last. The first paper carried a recap of the story that was on the news the night before and a picture of the Moore Towers from the ground floor shooting up. Not much information could be seen since, most of the damage occurred on the 11th floor and up. The second paper had a similar story; a little more detail oriented than the first but still didn't have any information as to what had transpired. The picture in this paper was taken of the window from where the shooter had fired. It appeared that the photographer had worked a deal with someone from my apartment building to take pictures out of his or her window.

Picking up the Times, plastered across the front-page of the paper was one of the pictures I had taken of the shooter. In addition to the picture was a lengthy article claiming there was a cover-up. I knew where this story was headed. I sat on the edge of the bed looking into the shooter's face trying to determine if I had ever seen his face before.

Again there was a knock at the door; this time there was someone there. I asked, "Who is it?"

He simply replied, "The Times."

I started to unlatch the door when my phone rang, I told the guy at the door that it would be just one minute, I moved across the room for the phone. I picked up the phone and it was John on the other end. He said, "Congratulations, looks like your story is going to check out, I will send a driver over for you immediately."

"You are falling behind of yourself," I replied. "The driver is at my door right now."

The phone line fell silent for a second then John said, "Do not open the door; my driver has not left yet. I will send my driver and several security officers. My spokesman will identify himself as Stevens. In the mean time I will call the hotel security and have the person at your door removed."

As fear of the impending situation gripped me I wondered why I had not taken the five thousand dollars. I also wondered why I even took the pictures; it was not like I needed the money. Additional knocking at the door, this time a little firmer than before interrupted my thoughts. I replied, "Just one more minute, I'm still on phone."

I began to look around the room for a place to hide. There was no place in this suite that would be a safe. I decided I better position myself so that I could have a chance to get the drop on this joker. I turned all the lights out except for the light in the hallway. I moved to the left wall facing the door in front of the hall. If this guy breaks in and he is holding a gun in his right hand I might be able to grab his arm. As I positioned myself against the wall I heard the sound of the door being kicked. I wasn't sure if the door held or not and couldn't afford to look around the corner to find out. My heart was beating in my throat and to think this is the life I use to live for. I was much younger then and getting hurt or killed never crossed my mind. I waited, listened and watched for any shadows to appear from of the hallway.

After what seemed to be an eternity there was another knock on the door followed by a voice, which said, "Stevens here."

I moved into the hallway and peered through the beep hole. In the hallway were four men, two were wearing security uniforms, one had an earpiece and the other must have been Stevens. I responded, "Who sent you?"

Stevens replied, "The Times."

"Specifically, who from the Times sent you," I insisted.

"Mr. John Clarkston, associate editor of the Times."

I unbolted the door, the two security guards pushed their way past Stevens and myself and went directly into the apartment. In passing one asked, "Are you alone?"

I couldn't resist taking a jab at the New York mentality and said, "No, you are here!"

The man in the suit reached in from the hallway of the hotel and grabbed my arm. He said, "Mr. Moore, it is imperative for your safety that you come with us now."

Without opportunity to respond I was pulled through the doorway and whisked to the awaiting elevator. At the elevator another man in a suit met us, I asked, "Stevens, is this man with you."

Stevens responded, "No, he is the elevator operator."

A brief moment of hesitation and Stevens said, "Yanking your chain, he is with us."

We got on the elevator and Stevens handed me a cellular phone. Almost instantly it rang, on the other end was John Clarkston. He said, "You will not be coming back to the Newspaper building, instead you are going to be taking in a roundabout way to a predetermined address that only the driver, Stevens and I know the final destination."

We got down to the parking garage and I was hurried into a sedan with the windows blacked out. The driver started the car and headed for down town New York City. I was given copies of the pictures, which I had taken and asked if I could identify any of the people in the pictures. Each of the pictures had captured the faces of the men, and enlarged them. Scanning the pictures, I did not notice any familiar faces.

MANHATTAN SHOOTING

My attention was redirected from the photos to the driver when he slammed on the brakes. Looking through the front windshield of the car I could see why we came to such a quick stop. There was a construction crew working on the road and traffic was backed up for several blocks. In an attempt not to be caught up in traffic the driver turned into the adjacent lane and headed up an alley. I looked behind our car and saw several cars, which followed the driver's lead. This is not an uncommon practice for New York City drivers.

Leaving the alley and returning to movement as usual, I turned my focus back to the photos. I scanned the remaining pictures and when I looked up all eyes were on me. Stevens asked, "Did you recognize anyone in the pictures?"

I replied, "No, as far as I know I have never seen the shooter or the other men except when I took their pictures. Of course this is the closest that I have had a chance to see them."

The car continued to change directions about every three to four blocks, never spending too much time going the same direction. I settled back into the seat and tried to enjoy the ride. Feeling a bit like a kid on a trip I turned to Stevens and asked, "How much longer will we be on the road?"

Stevens leaned in as though to whisper something in my ear and said, "Take a nap, read a magazine, or count cars, we are going to be on the road for quite a while."

Hours of travel and we finally pulled into a roadside dinner. The place was a grease trap for truckers. We went in and huddled into a booth in the middle of the dinner. I ordered a cheeseburger, fries and Pepsi. The waitress was quick to point out that only Coke was available. I replied, "Water will be fine."

When the remaining items were ordered I excused myself from the table and headed for the bathroom. Everyone at the table except the driver and Stevens accompanied me, I felt like a dangerous convict having my final meal. I finished my business and felt compelled to wash my hands. I wondered how the rest of these guys could hold it so long, it must have something to do with being a well trained fighting machine, or it could just be that they were all twenty years younger than I was.

We returned to the table and it wasn't long before the meals were delivered to the table. We ate and when the waitress noticed we were about to complete our meal she brought the receipt to the table and asked, "Who is the lucky recipient?"

Stevens said, "I guess I am and started to pull out a credit card." Shocked by Stevens' lack of knowledge of going underground I asked, "Is that your personal credit card?"

Stevens said, "No it is . . ."

I interrupted him before he could say it belonged to the newspaper and said to the waitress, "Could you give us just a moment to argue about who is paying for the meal?"

"Sure doll, just don't forget the tip," came her reply.

I looked at Stevens and said, "The first thing you have to do when you don't want to lead people to where you are at is don't leave clues. This is a cash meal; I hope you have it, because I only have five bucks in my pocket."

Stevens raised an eyebrow and said, "So you have been in hiding before?"

Without thinking I answered, "Not exactly hiding, but I do know how to minimize any paper trail to my whereabouts. The first thing you learn is that cellular phones are like sending a GPS signal to anyone that is trying to track you down. Using credit cards, talking about yourself to strangers or even bank accounts or Internet purchases will leave a paper trail to you."

The waitress moved back by the table and Stevens pulled a hundred dollar bill out of an envelope to pay for the meal. I thought if he had all that expense money why would he pull out a company credit card. I looked up at the waitress and joking said, "Keep the change!"

She flashed her eyes back to Stevens for confirmation from him and he said, "You heard the man, keep the change!"

Before I knew it the waitress had swooped down to my neck and gave me a big hug. I guess she thought I had something to do with her getting such a large tip. She hurried around the table to where Stevens was getting out of the booth and placed a big kiss on his cheek and gave him a bear hug. I laughed inside thinking how mad Stevens must be at me for costing him such a big tip.

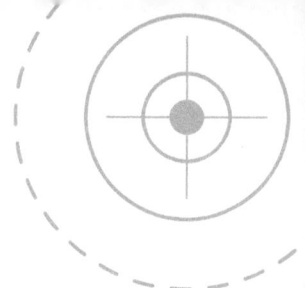

CHAPTER 6

SECLUSION

We reached the car and after we all settled in for the trip remaining Stevens slipped his hand inside his suit jacket and pulled out the envelope that he had paid the waitress from and extended it in my direction. With a huge grin smeared across his face he said, "Your expense money, spend it wisely, I am not sure when you will be receiving more."

I reached for the envelope and said; "I guess I should have got the kiss on the cheek from the waitress."

Everybody in the car including the stone-faced security guards began to laugh. I tried to hold back the laughter, but I eventually had to laugh, after all it is not every day that you tip larger than the cost of the meal. When the laughter died down to a controllable roar I said, "When we get to where we are going will any of you be staying with me?"

Stevens said, "Murphy and I will be staying with you. We have borrowed a car from a family member of one of the papers employees so the car can't be traced. See, for the most part we don't leave a paper trail."

I looked over at Stevens and said, "I am sorry if I offended you with the paper trail speech back at the diner. I guess I have read to many espionage novels. I am sure you are well trained to do your job of protecting me. Look this cloak-and-dagger stuff has me on edge, is there any way I could know your first names?"

Stevens responded, "James, my friends call me Jim, Murphy's first name is Mack. I spent the better part of the first year I knew him calling him McMurphy. One day a call came into the office and the lady asked to speak with Mack. I hesitated a minute, then assumed she was talking about McMurphy. I called over to him to let him know he had a call. Immediately I heard hysterical laughter coming from the other end of the receiver. Between the laughter she managed to say, 'you must be the guy that thinks Mack is part of Murphy's last name. We spend hours laughing about you calling him McMurphy.' When Murphy finally got to the phone I handed him the handset and said don't be long Mack."

Amused by the story I said, "Thanks Jim; McMurphy it is nice to meet you guys on a personal basis."

We traveled for several more hours and I could tell by the sun's travel we were heading south. I never mentioned anything more about when we were going to arrive. I had found that the time would pass much quicker if I engaged in reading. I read cover to cover the sports magazine that was in the back seat.

The car began to slow and I noticed the ride was a bit bumpy when Jim announced, "We were here."

The sun had already begun to set so I knew we were miles from New York. Jim and Mack pulled their luggage out of the trunk, then Mack handed me a bag. I asked, "You want me to be your bellhop?"

Mack smiled and replied, "It's yours, and we bought you a few things."

A turn of the key and a kick from Jim's heal and the cabin door swung open. There was a musky smell inside the cabin; you could tell at a glance that it had not been used in a while. I sat my luggage by the front door and began to explore the insides of the cabin with my eyes. It appeared to have one large living quarter down stairs, a small kitchen and probably a bathroom down the hall. The stairs moved up out of the main room. There were three doors and one hallway at the top of the stairs. Jim and Mack were still making trips back and forth to the trunk of the car. I asked, "Is there anything I can do to help?"

Jim handed me a box of kitchen supplies and said, "You can take this to the kitchen then see if you can figure out how to get the lights to work."

I sat the supplies on the counter and worked my way over to the light switch. I toggled the switch back and forth a couple of times with no luck. I started looking through the drawers in the kitchen for a flashlight to no avail. I walked down the hallway to the back of the cabin; it was larger than it appeared from the outside. There was a game room set up behind the kitchen complete with pool table and card table. I tried the switch, on and off, no light. I scanned the room for a breaker box. I decided the breakers must be on the outside of the cabin. I went back into the hallway and found another door. I tried to flip the switch, no dice. I looked in the closet for the breaker box, no luck. At the back door were several switches. I assumed one of them was for the outside lights the others were to control something inside the room. I left the cabin and on the back corner of the cabin was the box in which I had been searching. I opened the front panel and started throwing switches. The porch lights came on and illuminated the wooded area to the side of the cabin.

At the back door my curiosity got the better of me, why were there so many switches? I started flipping switches one at a time. The first turned the lights on in the room. I knew the second switch was for the porch lights. The third switch appeared to have no function. The final switch when toggled caused trail lights to illuminate down a path through the woods. Intrigued by the quest for adventure I followed the path. After a couple twist and turns I could see the boat dock. It too was illuminated. I walked out onto the dock and drew a deep breath from off the water. It was the first smog free breath I had taken in years. I almost forgot what it was like to spend any time away from the city.

I sat down at the end of the dock and watched as the setting sun light mirrored off the water's surface. It was a sight that only a country boy at heart could appreciate.

Startled by the sound of footsteps rushing up the dock in my direction, I turn to see Stevens, with gun drawn and a huge frown on his face. He said, "Have you lost your mind? Don't you know you should say something to us before you go traipsing off?"

Looking up at Stevens I said, "Settle down Jim, we are going to be spending a lot of time sitting here on this dock together; you might as well get use to it right now."

Stevens still frowning said, "I don't think so Chris, we have a lot of work to get done in the next few days. Let's get back to the cabin."

I accompanied Jim back to the cabin, when we arrived to the back of the cabin the car was pulling away. Mack was entering the front of the cabin as we entered the hall and he said, "I see you found him."

I replied, "It wasn't hard, I just followed the lights."

Not amused by my wit, Mack said, "Why don't you sit down, we will need to get some information from you?"

I pulled up one of the rustic chairs and sat down. *Funny how rustic and uncomfortable go hand in hand.* I sat there quietly while the two were in the kitchen putting things away. It was completely dark now and with the sun being down it didn't take long for the chill to set in. I asked, "Would it be alright if I built a fire?"

Murphy replied, "If you think you can do it without setting the whole place on fire."

I pulled some wood and kindling from the wood box and built a fire. The wood was seasoned and soon the fire was burning hot. I pulled the screen shut and backed away from the fire. The room was warm in no time. I was feeling quite accomplished until Mack called in, "When you get tired of playing, the thermostat is at the foot of the stairs!"

Glancing across the room to the stairwell I saw the thermostat on the wall. I wanted to come back with something like; I saw it but there is nothing like the smell of a fresh wood burning or something along those lines. I knew if I said anything that they would know they bested me, so I sat silent.

The cell phone that Jim was carrying rang. I immediately cautioned, "Don't answer it!"

Too late, I heard Jim say hello. I rushed into the kitchen where Mack was preparing supper and said, "Are you nuts, they can track you from that phone?"

Jim covered the receiver and said, "Settle down Chris, it is secure."

I could not figure how any cellular phone could be secure. I was busting a seam to continue this argument about a secure cell phone. While I was fuming and waiting the opportunity to resume our discussion Jim hands me the phone and said, "He wants to talk with you."

Still antsy about using a cell phone I took it from Jim's outstretched arm and answered. It was John on the other end. He started his conversation with an apology. When I enquired for what, he began his story. "The research group for the newspaper went a little overboard on background checks, especially yours. Let me start from the beginning. The shooter and the men in his room all work for covert groups of the government. It seems one of them had picked up on the fact that the only way he could retire was if someone older than he had passed away to make an opening in their protection program. It appears budget cuts were the cause for this."

I found a chair to sit in and asked, "You mean I was the target all along."

John said, "I guess that would be a good summary."

"What are you going to do? Are you still going to run the story?"

"Well, yes and no, the agency has given us the story we are going to run. It is not the Pulitzer Prize story we thought we had, but it will still sell papers, of course not to the tune of two hundred and fifty thousand dollars."

"So Mr. Clarkston I guess we're no longer on a first name basis."

"Of course we are still on a first name basis; as a matter of fact you are more interesting to me now than before. I want to do your story," John insisted.

"I don't have a story. My story days are long since past memories. It has been over ten years since I even had a mission."

"That doesn't mean the public don't have a right to know about the operations which go on under their noses."

"I disagree with that form of thinking. If the public knew a UFO crashed in Roswell and the technology that was gained from that crash built the electronics revolution don't you think they would like to know at what expense this information cost them?"

John said, "What are you talking about, your agency had nothing to do with UFOs?"

"I am aware of what my agency was in charge of, but I don't think the public would care to know at what expense to them my agency is allowed to operate. That was the message I was trying to convey with the UFO cover-up story."

"Well Chris, it is your decision to make. Your old agency has asked me to tell you that you are called back in. So it is up to you whether you go back to them or let us continue to hide you and you expose the agency."

"John that is out of the question, my life wouldn't be worth a plugged nickel if I exposed the agency."

John replied, "What do you think it will be worth if you go back in? Don't make a decision tonight; I will be in contact with you again."

As I pressed end on the phone John's question echoed in my head, what will my life be worth if I go back in?"

I knew I had to make a decision, but exposing the agency I worked for was not the right decision. I was trying to run all the options through my head when Jim interrupted, "The phone is secure because we bought it with cash and paid for the minutes in cash. When the time has expired we will throw the phone away and pay cash for another."

I smiled at Jim and said; "I told you I had confidence in your ability to keep me safe. What are your qualifications?"

"I spent seven years in the special forces, eight more working as an operative for the CIA, and the past five years as head of security for the newspaper."

"I hate to admit it but against the team you wouldn't last ten minutes. Those guys are like junk yard dogs, if you knock them down they get back up and keep coming."

"Don't underestimate me; two of the eight years I was with the CIA, I trained with an elite guard unit."

"I'm sorry Jim; I have a hard time judging anybody these days. You get to thinking you're on top of the game when the truth is the game has gone off and left you. I forget I am not in my twenties or thirties any more. My mind is as sharp as it was back then, but my body feels aches that it never uses to recognize."

Mack moved into the living room and joined the conversation by saying, "I understand about misjudging people, I was under the impression you were some pansy freelance, I had no idea that you had spent time with the agency."

"At one time, I was a top agent, now that I have lost a step; it would be like Jim Brown suiting up to play football again. It would be exciting but I am afraid he wouldn't make many yards."

Mack replied, "You lose your edge when you find out that you are not invincible."

I then looked at Mack and asked, "Do you have any background training that qualifies you to protect me?"

Mack answered, "Not really, I was a Marine for seven years, my specialty was explosives, and however, I am a marksman and did qualify as a sniper but that life is way too boring for me. You don't get to blow anything up. I spent some time as a mercenary but never really got any satisfaction out of working for causes I didn't believe in."

We continued our bonding well into the night. I looked at my wristwatch and noticed it was getting close to two in the morning and suggested we get some rest. Mack and Jim headed up to their rooms and I found my luggage and followed.

The bed was unmade but the linen was placed at the foot of the bed. I made the bed, showered, shaved and brushed my teeth. Looking through the contents of my luggage I was shocked to find a 9mm and a shoulder harness in with my clothing. Oh well, too late tonight to get any answers, it will keep until the morning.

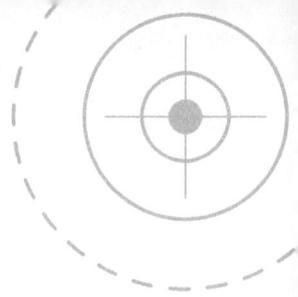

CHAPTER 7

THE SIEGE

I awoke the following morning to a loud cracking noise; instinctively I reached for the 9mm and headed for the sound. I crouched down by the door and pulled the door inward enough to see the stairs then I waited and listened. I heard the noise again, shut the door and freshened up for the upcoming day. When I was dressed I decided to strap on the shoulder harness and see if anybody noticed.

When I got down stairs I started frying bacon and put on a pot of coffee. The smell of the bacon soon filled the cabin and it wasn't too long after that my would-be protectors put down their pool cues and came into the kitchen. I replied, "Kind of scary to be woke up by the sound of balls cracking together."

Both men prepared to apologize when I said, "Good thing I had my trusty pea shooter." (Patting the 9mm)

"Oh about the gun, it helps to have a friend at the paper. Mr. Clarkston arranged with the President for your new identity cover to be that of a Federal Marshal. All the documentation is in my room in my brief case," explained Stevens.

"Being a Federal Marshal is a little too high profile of a cover for me. I would rather move to Texas and become a rancher."

"I know you would, but the President said he needs you to expose your old unit," Jim said.

"Expose my unit, I find it hard to believe that the President would make such a request."

Jim replied, "Seems they are no longer operating as a Federal unit, they have gone private. They have become a threat to homeland security. You can expect a call from the President by three o'clock today, so you can hear everything for yourself firsthand."

"I can't believe the President would want me to expose the unit, no matter how they are operating now, they were a covert group for the government at one time. Besides that, I have several friends that were still active in the organization. There has to be another way."

Mack spoke up, "Your friends aren't worried about you being exposed. They are trying to kill you."

"I need to get some air, I think I will take a walk down to the docks." I grabbed some bacon, a piece of toast and a cup of coffee and headed for the door.

"We can all use some air, we will go with you," Jim replied.

Outside the cabin, Mack attached an alarm to the outside of the back door. I chuckled when I saw what he had done, thinking *boy that will stop someone from going back into the cabin*. We walked on the trail that led to the boat dock and when we came to the final turn in the trail Jim reached for my shoulder and stopped me. He motioned for me to stop and said, "Let me check out the dock."

Jim must really get off on the cloak-and-dagger stuff. He slipped around the bend in the trail as Mack and I watched him until he was out of sight. Mack said, "He is really being cautious."

I laughed aloud, "He is being cautious, what about you and the external alarm I saw you setting on the back door of the cabin?"

Mack looked serious and said, "Alarm, that was no alarm, it was C4, if someone other than me tries to open that door or remove the C4 it blows up."

"Great, what if something were to happen to you, how would we get back into the cabin?"

"In little pieces if you insist on using the back door," Mack said with a smile.

Jim rejoined us on the trail and said, "Everything is clear, let's go."

"Jim, why wouldn't everything be clear, you didn't put an advertisement in the paper announcing we were coming to a cabin in the woods did you?"

"No, but you can never be too cautious. The first time you let down your guard may be your last time in this business."

I smiled inwardly at their zeal and walked out to the front of the dock and sat down. I liked the way the breeze felt coming in off of the lake. It was such a tranquil environment that it caused you to quickly forget all your cares. I began to think back to my high school days of playing football and baseball. I remembered the good times I spent on the water fishing with my father, my uncles and my granddad. Those were good times, not a care in the world. I thought back to the girls I had dated in high school and wondered what had become of them. I hadn't seen any of them since I graduated in what seemed to be a lifetime ago. Jim sat down next to me and said, "Chris, you are a long ways off aren't you."

Without even interrupting my daydream I said, "All the way back to high school."

I heard him begin to chuckle, then, as my daydream resurfaced in my head, his chuckles faded. I was back among family and friends. I never realized how much I missed the simple life until right about now. As a young man that sort of life bored me and I couldn't wait to get out of town. I often wondered how my parents could stand to live so isolated from everyone else. I wondered why my friends stayed around that small town. The next sound I heard was an explosion back up the trail; this shook me from my daydream permanently.

Jim gripped my arm and said, "Stay here, Mack and I will take care of this."

Mack was waiting at the front of the dock and he said, "Hey Chris, Pretty good alarm system after all!"

Mack and Jim headed up the trail. I knew they were going to need my help. I pulled my 9mm and headed into the woods. I found my skills of staying out of sight instinctively returned. I could still see Mack and Jim were remaining on the trail. I was wondering when they were going to get off the trail and take cover in the woods. I didn't have time to worry about them as I noticed some movement by the cabin. I crouched behind a fallen tree and strained to catch another glimpse. Another hazard of getting old, your eagle vision seems to slip. I shed my white shirt and crawled along through the underbrush until I could see the corner of the cabin that the breaker box was on. I wasn't sure if anyone was in the cabin. I stayed still and surveyed the area. I was afraid that whoever had come after us might have infrared scanners and if so they could be trained on me right now. If this were a team, it would either be two or four men; in either case I figure they were one man short. (The guy that tried entering through the back door.)

I couldn't identify any movement, so I began to reposition myself to the front of the cabin. I moved about sixty yards beyond the front of the cabin before I started to close in on the lane. I moved close enough to see a black SUV parked on up the lane. I decided to see if anyone was watching from the truck. I moved close enough to see inside, it was empty. I decided to wait there, if Mack and Jim weren't as good as they thought the agents would come back to their vehicle sooner or later. I waited, I heard a burst from an automatic weapon, and I assumed Jim or Mack one was eliminated. I listened for return fire and heard nothing.

I waited for about two hours and there were no additional shots fired. I feared that maybe Mack and Jim were grouped during that initial burst and both men were killed or even worse, one was dead and the other surrendered. I figured whichever scenario was correct; the agents were looking for me.

I slowly worked my way down the lane towards the cabin. When I was close enough to see the cabin I climbed up into a pine tree. I climbed slowly as to not knock any bark off the branches. I reached about thirty feet off the ground and looked down to make sure there were plenty of branches to block a direct view of me. I sprawled out onto a branch so that I could lie down to view the cabin and I began to watch. I briefly saw some movement inside the cabin, in what had been my room. I watched the area, no more signs of movement. About three hours had passed when I heard the pine needles below my tree stir. I had a sick feeling in my stomach that I had been seen and was fixing to be shot. I lie motionless except for my eyes; I was scanning for an opening through to the ground. Finally I noticed an opening on the north side of the tree, so I focused on that spot. Minutes passed and I saw a figure moving away from the cabin towards the SUV. Judging from his build and the way he held himself it appeared to be Mack. I couldn't be positive and if it was Mack I didn't want to spook him and get shot accidentally.

When the figure had moved far enough into the woods that I knew he wouldn't hear me, I began to work my way down out of the tree. Around fifteen feet from the ground I could see the top of the SUV. It moved as though someone was getting in or out of the vehicle. I waited and watched, minutes later I saw Mack walking in the lane towards the cabin. I was getting ready to call to him when I heard another voice ask, "Have you found him?"

I froze, I couldn't tell if the other voice was that of Jim or not. I wasn't sure if I was being paranoid or not, but for now I was going to remain in hiding until I could positively identify the voice. I waited until they had moved closer to the cabin, when they reached a bend in the lane I climbed out of the tree. I started moving closer to the cabin, staying just inside the woods, as to not become an easy target. I was gaining ground on them, neither had their weapons pulled and neither was acting as though they were in danger. I slipped up close enough to get bits and pieces of their conversation. Still unsure what to do I just waited and listened until I noticed Jim's profile as he turned towards Mack.

Relieved but still cautious I stepped out into the open gripping my 9mm and said, "Enjoying your walk."

Jim whirled around; his shocked look quickly changed to a smile and he said, "Glad to see you made it. We had almost decided you had gotten lost."

I asked, "So how many agents were there?"

Mack replied, "Only two, I got one and the other is all over the back of the cabin."

Still trying to figure things out in my head the phone rings. Jim says, "Must be three o'clock."

I glanced at my watch, three o'clock it was. Jim pitched the phone to me and said, "It's for you. We will be waiting inside."

"No, wait, we will all go together, I still have some questions."

I answered the phone, it was the President, and he explained the situation with my old outfit turning mercenary. I was having a hard time buying that some of the guys I served with would ever turn their backs on our country. I made a few individual enquires about some of my closest friends. Most were dead or unaccounted for. Seems when the group went renegade, the non-followers were being eliminated and I was on the non-follower list. After all my questions were answered the President went on to explain why he had assigned me the position of Federal Marshal. I told him about my quarter of a million dollars I expected to collect from the newspaper and he said there would be no problems if I agreed to the terms of my new contract with Uncle Sam.

When I got off the phone I had entirely too much on my mind to deal with two guys I wasn't sure I could trust. I asked, "Who shot the agent?"

Mack smiled and said, "I did."

I asked if I could see his gun, Mack said, "Why it is just like yours?"

With this admission, I pointed my gun at both of them and ordered they drop their guns. Mack complied immediately, but Jim was a bit hesitant. I called out to Jim, "Do it now or die!"

Jim reached inside his jacket and pulled his pistol from its holster and sat it on the ground then asked, "What is this all about?"

I ordered them both to put their hands on their heads and take several steps forward. I then explained, "When I was moving into position to check out the agent's vehicle I heard a burst from a quick firing weapon, neither of you have a quick firing weapon."

"Oh, is that all? Mack's Uzi is inside," Jim insisted.

I turned to Mack, "Why were you coming from up the lane?"

Mack replied, "I knew they had to have driven here and there was a black Expedition just around that bend."

I asked Mack "Was anyone there? *Remembering the SUV moved as someone got in or out of it earlier.*

Mack replied, "No, I even got inside to check and see if there were any radios or weapons remaining in the thing."

Mack's story checked out. I asked Jim if anyone was inside the cabin earlier. He said, "Sure, when we got to the top of the trail, I covered Mack as he went in through the back door. He then covered me as I entered the cabin. We did a quick search down stairs, and then went directly up stairs to our rooms to get our heavy weapons. I pulled my sniper rifle with infrared scope and Mack pulled his Uzi. We both checked your room then went back to Mack's room to check the dock with the scope to make sure you were all right. It was then that I spotted the intruder just off the trail. As soon as I was sure it wasn't you I spotted for Mack. Mack fired one quick burst and got him. I watched him through the infrared scope as his body heat faded before we went down to check and make sure he was dead. Mack went down and verified he was dead, drug his body onto the trail then came back to me, while I watched to make sure Mack didn't get jumped. After one last scan of the cabin, we went down to the dock to get you and you were gone. Mack tracked your footprints to the SUV then lost you on the way back to the cabin. We were about to start calling your name when you showed up."

I pulled the clips out of their pistols and handed them back to them. I said, "I am sorry, but it is my life which is on the line right now and I only trust me for the time being. Holster your pistols without the clips, which leave each of you one shot. When we check out your story I will return your clips."

Jim was outwardly angry because of my distrust of him but Mack seemed to understand. We worked our way back to the cabin. As we neared the cabin, Mack reached inside his jacket and pulled out my shirt and said, "Here you might want to put this back on."

I took my shirt and as we passed through the cabin, the remains of the agent that attempted to open the back door were exactly where Mack said they would be, scattered. As we walked the trail towards the dock, I noticed the body; I stooped to check for identification. He had the standard organization cover paperwork in his wallet. I pulled the keys to the Expedition from his pocket and then called the local police to report the bodies.

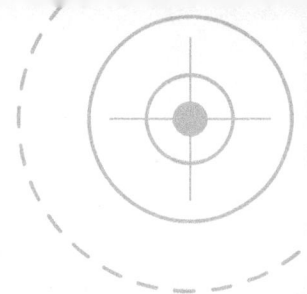

CHAPTER 8

COVER UP

I extended my hand with the clips for their pistols towards Jim and Mack and said, "Before the police arrive, I don't plan on being here. Let's get our stuff together, wipe the place down and hit the road. Grab some non-perishable foods, your bags and I will meet you out front in the Expedition."

Jim took his clip and without responding spun away and headed for the cabin. Mack said, "Don't worry Chris, he really took a liking to you and it hurt his feelings that you didn't trust him. I understand, you don't know either of us well enough to trust us with your life."

I smiled at Mack and said, "Thanks, I had no idea that my whole life was going to be turned upside down over this situation. I thought I would make a few bucks selling a few pictures and that would be that. I never thought for one minute that I was the shooter's target."

Heading down the stairs with my luggage I called back into Mack and Jim, "I will be in the Expedition waiting, but not for long, I want to be out of here before we have to answer any questions."

I hiked up the lane for the SUV, I figured this vehicle would have GPS tracking, but I also figured if it sat in one place too long that a second team would be dispatched. So I decided to use the tracking device against the agency. If I took the SUV out on the road the agent tracking the SUV would either think that the team had completed their mission or that we had taken the SUV and a team could be dispatched when we got close enough for them to reach us overnight.

When I approached the cabin, Jim and Mack were out front with their luggage. The SUV was loaded quickly and we were on our way. After reaching the main road and driving several miles beyond the turn off for the cabin I pulled off the road. "One of you guys can take over the driving, I want to look over my paperwork and decide what to do next."

Mack got out of the back seat and opened the driver's side door and said, "I'll drive but you will have to let me know where we are going."

I said, "For now, let's just drive."

I got my paperwork from Jim and began studying my new identity. I was to become Michael Sloan, a member of law enforcement for the past twenty years. This seemed to be obtainable enough cover; after all I did like donuts.

We drove until dark, putting some distance between the cabin and us. We grew tired of snacking on pretzels and drinking bottled water, so we pulled into a restaurant. Inside we placed our orders and began to plan our next step. In the middle of explaining what my objectives were as dictated by the President, Jim said, "I am not sure if you can start your new job until you are finished with your business with the paper."

I looked into Jim's eyes and replied, "Of course I can start my new job, I already have and Mack and you both helped. There are only about fifty more people to get out of the way."

Mack interrupted, "Our job is to keep you safe until the newspaper tells us different."

We finished our meals and on the way out I picked up a copy of the Times. In the SUV I began to read the headlines. *'AGENT WANTED BY POLICE FOR QUESTIONING'* At first I thought I had been betrayed by John Clarkston, but after reading the rest of the story and seeing the picture of the shooter I realized John was running my story as promised.

The police had found our little surprise and were beginning to broadcast the story on the air. Their version of the truth was much different than we had anticipated. The official story they released claimed the two men were killed in a car crash on the lane instead of by gunshot wound and an explosion. When the story on the radio had finished Mack said, "Do you think it was the two assassins we killed that the story was about or could there possibly be two other men killed?"

I replied, "It is the typical cover story when an agent falls. The problem is the government is the one that leaks the official version of the story. Someone in the administration is still covering the agency's activities. If I am supposed to shut the group down, I will need to know who is creating their cover stories."

Jim immediately got on the phone began explaining our need for finding out who inside the government is covering for the agency. He spent about ten minutes filling John in on the events of the day.

We were running low on gas and Mack was getting tired from driving. He said, "I can use a break from driving and we are almost out of gas."

When I worked with the agency if I needed something I dialed a number, entered my code and was connected with someone within the agency that made decisions. If I needed money, a car, or a new cover story I just called in and it happened. Now that I am working direct for the President, I am not sure how or who to contact for supplies. Supplies suddenly became very important.

I decided it was time to explain to Jim and Mack how dangerous things were going to be in the near future. I waited until we had pulled over for refueling. When the gas was pumped and we had reached the edge of town I instructed Mack to pull over. We pulled into a roadside park and I began, "You guys have been great, you protected me like true professionals, but it is time for us to part ways."

Jim exclaimed, "We are assigned to protect you and until our orders change that is what we are going to do!"

I smiled at Jim and replied, "Jim, that is very commendable and I appreciate your dedication, and however, you do not know how these guys operate. I will have a hard enough time dodging these clowns without worrying about your safety. I have to drive to the warehouse district in Plano, Texas, break into a warehouse and steal the things I need to level the playing field with the agency. I also have to get there before the agency realizes I am coming. I found out about the warehouse totally by mistake over eight years ago, seems someone in the shipping department was lax in his or her job and left the original invoice tucked inside one of my kits with the warehouse's address on the invoice. This warehouse is supposed to be top secret."

Jim replied, "Then we had better get started for Texas."

Mack replied, "Not in this truck, I am sure there must be some type of tracking device attached to this vehicle if it belongs to the government."

"That's right, we will have to get a different vehicle, one that can't be tracked, or at least one that no one knows we have, so even if it is tracked, they won't know we are in it," I stated.

Mack said, "Let's go shopping Chris, or . . . ah . . . I mean, Mike. I think I will call you Mike instead of Michael."

I smiled at Mack because he remembered my new cover, then I said, "I am going to get another vehicle but you two aren't coming along. There is too much risk and I operate better alone."

Jim replied, "Not this time Mike, we have your back. Besides if we let you get away we would lose our jobs with the paper. I know you wouldn't want that."

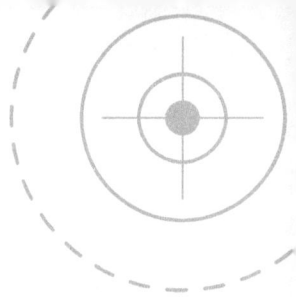

CHAPTER 9

ROAD TRIP

Inwardly pleased with their insistence to help I replied, "You can come along but we will be breaking some laws. I am protected with my Federal Marshal status but you guys will be at the mercy of some judge."

Both Mack and Jim sat silent for a minute then Mack said, "Not if you deputize us, wouldn't we become Federal Deputies?"

I thought for a minute and said, "I guess that might work."

With all this being settled we got back on the road, Jim had taken over the driving duties. I told Jim to drive to the nearest used car dealership. We found a dealership that had a 2000 model F150 with four-doors parked out in front. I told Jim to drive passed the dealership to the nearest restaurant, he did. I got out and told them to order me a cheeseburger and chocolate shake, and then I started walking back up the road towards the dealership.

I paid cash for the truck and had the title put in the name of Tom Smith. As I approached the restaurant I saw Jim and Mack getting back into the SUV, I pulled alongside of them and got my cheeseburger and drink and told them to follow me. We headed north out of town. We drove for about two hours until I saw a road sign pointing off the road to a small town.

We pulled into the town, it was one of those towns that the sidewalks roll up at five o'clock and the only excitement in town is what is broadcast on the television. I pulled into a dealership on the out skirts of town and parked. Jim pulled up behind me and I told them to move the luggage over. I got out, opened the bed cover on the pickup to store our luggage then headed for the SUV.

After the transfer was complete and the interior and exterior of the SUV were wiped of prints, I got into the truck and said, "If we drive all night and into the day tomorrow we can make it to Plano by dark. Are you ready to see Texas?"

Mack replied, "I guess I will try and get some sleep, I will spell you when you get ready for me to drive."

Jim and I began to talk about what to expect when dealing with the agency. I explained how the teams worked an assignment. The two men teams' works cover type operations. Only one agent exposes himself to harm's way while the other agent holds back to lie down retreat cover incase the situation turns bad. These agents are trained to eliminate up to five hostiles at one time and escape without being harmed. The four men teams are made up of one sniper, one spotter, and two leads. The leads are used to pull the target into the open, the spotter assesses the hit sight to make sure no one witnesses the hit and the sniper of course takes the shot or shots as needed. Jim asked, "How do you beat one of these teams?"

I replied, "You either get lucky like we did at the cabin or you out plan the team. If Mack had not set the charge on the door we would not have come through that siege so cleanly. Someone would have got hurt."

I decided if Jim and Mack were going to be working with me, then we would have to build a team of our own. I explained to Jim the importance of breaking into the warehouse undetected, not because I didn't want any confrontation but because a confrontation would involve people that were not members of the agency. We began to brainstorm different methods of entering and exiting the warehouse undetected. Mack had awaked from his slumber and began listening to our conversation and said, "Why not just show the person at the door your badge and tell them it is a federal search?"

I replied, "Good idea Mack, except the door man would log my name down and then my cover would be blown before I even got to use it."

We continued to bat around idea after idea shooting holes in each one as they were thrown out. Finally we hit on an idea that no matter how we tried to play the devil's advocate we could not find flaw. Our plan was to arrive at the warehouse district, find the building, then drive into the city and spend the night. The next morning we were going to the city planner's office and pull plans on nine of the warehouse buildings in the area, using the cover of building inspectors. I had used that cover in the past and found that the tax people try and stay out of the way of inspectors. When the plans for the warehouse had been studied we should be able to toggle the power to the warehouse several times causing the security alarms to sound. Each time we will attempt entry at a different place in the building. While inside the building we will continue to interrupt power until the security system is finally disabled. We will also monitor all outgoing calls to ensure our team is not detected and reported. The plan seemed foolproof; the test would be in the execution of the plan.

As we neared the Oklahoma border we pulled over and ate. I wasn't concerned about the travel money we had spent to this point but it was obvious this money was not going to last forever. We had about three thousand dollars left; this had to last us until we could surface again without fear of being shot. During the middle of the meal Mack commented, "Do you think you will be physically able to sneak into the warehouse and find the supplies you need and get out without being detected?"

I dropped the fork from my hand and said, "I am getting older but I think I can manage a simple assignment like breaking into a low guard area and pull the equipment we need, carry it out, all without getting caught."

Mack lowered his eyes and said, "I just wanted to check, because I think I could get in and out if you needed me to."

I smiled at Mack and replied, "Mack, you are a good man. I understand your concerns for a man of my age, but this is the type of job I am trained to do. I was not just an assassin trained to eliminate a target; I was trained to be stealth and creative. I could walk circles around a CIA operative and never be seen."

Mack frowned and said, "I just wanted to make sure, our job depends on you getting in and out untouched."

"I understand your concerns and would be the first to ask for help if I felt I wasn't the most qualified to complete this task. Now eat your supper, it is your turn to drive."

When we reached the truck I got in on the passenger side, Jim slid into the back seat and Mack the driver's seat. We had only been on the road about an hour when the Oklahoma state police pulled Mack over. The young officer was a real no nonsense type of guy. He came to the window and said, "I need proof of insurance and drivers license."

Mack began to comply when I interrupted. I said, "Officer this is my vehicle and I would like to have some words with you at your car."

The officer was not swayed and said, "You are not driving, and my business is with the driver." Turning back to Mack the officer said, "Now may I see your driver's license and proof of insurance"?

I was more insistent this time and said, "Officer, I am a Federal Marshal and must insist that you step down. You and I will have a private conversation and clear this matter up."

The officer reacted as though his agenda was more important than mine for a second then said, "OK step out of the car, keep your hands where I can see them."

I complied with his orders; I got out of the truck with my hands slightly above my shoulders. We moved to the back of the truck and he said, "Show me your identification."

I pulled my badge and wallet out. I handed him my identification card and began to explain, "We are on a mission assigned by the President and cannot risk having our cover blown. I have full rights to use these highways however I see fit. This of course includes speeding."

The young officer unsure of what action to take looked puzzled after my explanation. I said, "It is a professional courtesy that I am looking for, I can't afford for you to call this in and you feel it is your duty to make that call. Am I right so far"?

The young officer nodded then said, "If I let you go and you are some sort of felon and I didn't make the arrest then I would be the goat here."

"I understand your position, now you need to understand mine. I have a choice to make here as well, either I let you blow my cover or I stop you with whatever means are necessary. I do not want to get into a standoff situation with you; you are young, appear to have intelligence and should have a long future in law enforcement. If I were you I would not jeopardize your future with the police force nor would I jeopardize the mission I am on."

The young officer took up a defensive stance and said, "You are asking me to trust you and I don't even know who you are."

"I understand your predicament, honest I do, but you have to decide what you intend to do in the next fifteen seconds. That is all the time I can spare."

The young officer appeared torn on his decision when I explained, "The only problem we are going to have here is if you decide to call this in or report it later. If my cover gets blown, I will see to it that your career in law enforcement is over, I may even recommend charges be brought against you for obstruction."

With that being said, I reached out my hand for my wallet and badge. The young officer extended them towards me and said, "I trust you, don't let me down."

I climbed back into the truck; Mack and Jim were waiting to see what had happened and I said, "Let's go, we are burning time."

Mack pulled away from the shoulder of the road and insisted, "What did you say to get us out of the ticket?"

"I used my twenty years of law enforcement skills and power of persuasion to convince the officer that letting us go was the right thing to do."

Jim interrupted, "You don't have twenty years of law enforcement skills that is just your cover!"

"Oh yea, I forgot, hmmm, maybe I have a knack for this Federal Marshal stuff after all."

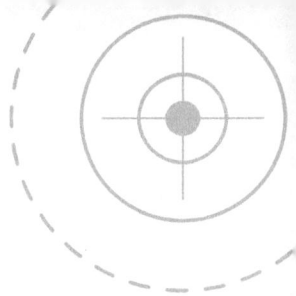

CHAPTER 10

RECON BEGINS

Around five hours later we pulled into the warehouse district in Plano. We drove to the warehouse that we had targeted for supplies and made a quick surveillance of the area. Only three vehicles were in the parking lot, which meant no more than six security guards. We drove the different routes through the warehouse district to ensure we had a clear route for escape in case something did go wrong. When we were confident that we had learned each possible escape route we headed for downtown.

We stopped and picked up pizza and found a motel for the night. Immediately we began to plan our events of the next day. We were going to pick up the plans for the building, find the various points of entry and focus on our break in. This was the first time that Mack had ever worked this type of mission. He said, "I am not sure how effective I will be, I don't think I have ever committed a crime in my life."

I replied, "Mack don't look at this as being a crime, look at this as making a withdraw from your own bank account. The material in the warehouse belongs to the Federal Government; we are working for the Federal Government and need the material inside the warehouse to complete our mission."

Jim added, "Besides you won't have to do anything except drive and listen to outgoing phone conversations."

The following morning Jim and I left Mack at the motel room and headed for the county tax assessors' office in Dallas. It was a longer drive than I had anticipated; when we reached the assessors' office we went in and read off the list of drawings that we needed. The lady at the counter went to the files and pulled the prints. She told us that it was going to be thirty dollars a print. We agreed and she went to make copies. When she got back with the copies she explained that two of the drawings we had requested were out for modifications. After looking through the drawings she provided us we were delighted to see our building was among the prints provided. We explained to her that we would be back later for the other two drawings, paid her and left.

In the truck Jim said, "That went way too smooth!"

I replied, "It went according to plan that is why you spend the time planning to ensure your odds for success are greater than the odds of failure. We were direct, acted as though we were supposed to be there and she bought it."

Jim said, "Why don't we just tell the guards that we are building inspectors and go into the warehouse the same way?"

"Do you think that the guards are just going to trust us and let us walk right inside a top secret government storage?"

Jim smiled and said, "If they don't we could fine them for not being up to code."

"Jim you are beginning to scare me with your play acting skills, you are acting aren't you?"

We both laughed and headed back for the motel. When we arrived at the motel, Mack had already taken care of breakfast. He had gone to the lobby and raided the buffet. There was enough food to feed six men. I looked at Mack and said, "I thought you said you had never stolen anything."

Mack with a shocked look on his face said, "I didn't steal this, the sign out front said the continental breakfast is complimentary."

We studied the plans of the warehouse and found there were at least nine different ways to access the warehouse. The two most likely areas to enter the building were from the roof. There were no external ladders to gain access to the roof so we had to figure out how we were going to be able to get on and off the roof. This would require finding a ladder that wouldn't be noticed. Then the idea came to me; why not use the cover of electrical repairmen. Not only could we gain access to the building by using the ladder but also we would have the perfect cover story to explain the electrical outage. This meant we were going to have to break into the electrical company and steal a truck with a ladder.

We went down town and located the electric company. In the electric company parking lot were the trucks we needed. Jim and I went to the front door and asked to see a supervisor; I showed him my badge and identification and explained to him that we suspected the warehouse to be a drug distribution center but needed to do some surveillance before we could get a warrant and make a bust. I asked to be allowed to borrow a truck. Too my surprise, the supervisor not only agreed to loan us a truck he provided us with jumpsuits, badges and a driver. He also explained that he would call several different warehouses including the warehouse we were interested in and notify them that their truck was going to be in the area working on the power. He instructed his driver to interrupt power as often as we needed.

This was too easy, I told the driver we had to sneak into the warehouse, gain some evidence then we would go back for the bust. He seemed more than willing to help us with the plan. Our plan was simple. The ladder would have to be raised, I would need to be dropped off on the roof and then the power would need to be toggled several times until I returned to the roof. The schedule for the power being toggled was simple, off for three minutes, back on for a minute, and then continue until the operation was complete.

When we reached the warehouse, Jim went to the front door to notify the guard that we were working on the power. He told them that the power would have to be interrupted several times. During his efforts to distract the guards, I was raised to the roof in the ladder truck. I stepped on the roof and got into position, I signaled the lineman to toggle power. When the power was turned off I pulled the vent fan cover. I signaled for the power to be turned back on. I expected to hear an alarm letting the guards know that the fan had been tampered with. There was no alarm, I signaled for the power to be turned off again for three minutes, toggled on for a minute then back off again for three minutes until I returned to the roof.

The plan worked perfect, I entered through the vent opening and found my way to the top of the warehouse pallet shelves which reached within two foot of the ceiling. This was almost too perfect. I located a pallet marked night vision, inside were boxes of night vision goggles. I pulled a pair from the pallet and put them on. It was a though someone had turned the lights on. I managed to reach the third level from the ground when the lights came back on. I hid between the pallets and waited, when the lights went off the next time I climbed down to the ground level and began to look. After several minutes of dodging forklifts I found what I had came for. There were briefcases already made up for field agents, tracking devices, IR scanners, timers and explosives, US currency and most important a snipers rifle. I pulled four cases and just as I began to climb the lights came back on. This time I was totally exposed for anyone or any cameras to see. I swung into the pallet shelves and hid. I watched my watch impatiently until the minute had ticked off. The lights again were off and I began to hurry back to the shelves that led to my escape.

When I arrived at the shelves there was a guard at either end of the shelves with flashlights. I moved to the middle of the adjacent shelves and climbed to the forth level. My three minutes were running out and I needed to find a place to hide. The pallet that I hid on began to creek under my weight. As the lights came back on the guards had already began to move in my direction.

The lights went out again and none too soon, the guards were zeroing in on my location. I moved vertically as soon as the lights went out. I had reached the inner part of the shelves and was able to place my feet on the support grids rather than the actual pallets. I moved to the end of the row before climbing to the ground and then back up on the next shelves. I slipped the four cases through the opening in the roof just as the lights came back on. I reached into the pallet with the night vision goggles and extracted four additional pairs. I climbed out of the vent and motioned for the linesman to kill the power and move back over in position to pick me up. I replaced the vent cover and secured it.

When the ladder had maneuvered me safely back to the ground, I instructed the linesman to continue disrupting power for at least twenty additional minutes. He raised his ladder back to the top of the power pole and continued cycling power. Jim had come over to assist me with the cases; the cameras which were set up in the parking lot were sweeping slowly right to left. We stood beside a panel van until the cameras began to sweep the parking lot and moved towards the pickup undetected. When we got to the pickup I got in the backseat with the cases and said, "Let's hit the road."

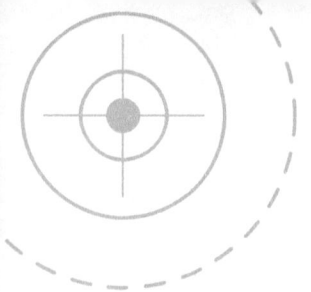

CHAPTER 11

THE TRAP

Unsure of what action to take, we decided to head into Dallas. When we reached Dallas we rented a hotel room and began planning. We had to be able to pull teams in one at a time and we had to be able to eliminate these teams without casualties. Mack got on the phone to John Clarkston to find out who was leaking the disinformation in Washington D.C. The leak was coming from a CIA official; he was Larry Brown, an old team member of mine. This knowledge would serve us well; we could monitor reports from his office and determine what action was going to be taken next.

We spent most of the night working on the details of our plan. We would go to a remote location with easy access and lead a team into us. The way we had planned to do this was to purposely leave a paper trail. We decided that if we drove down Interstate 20 until we came to a small enough towns that we could set up our web.

Our planning was complete; we were going to be able to pull a team in. The next morning we drove to Fort Worth and used a credit card to purchase gas. This was the beginning of our paper trail. We headed west on I-20 until we reached a town named Ranger. At Ranger I used a credit card again to pay for fountain drinks.

We pulled into the small town of Baird about an hour and a half later. It was the perfect place to set up our trap. The town was just off the interstate on old highway 80. The main street of town was about three blocks long. Antiques stores filled the town. We spread some money in a couple of the stores; the purchases of course were made with credit. We found a restaurant, which actually served some great barbeque. We went back out to the edge of town and rented a motel room. The room was facing the highway. This was going to be an advantage to us; we could monitor any traffic that entered the area.

We all took a briefcase and opened it. The cases were exactly alike, each contained two thousand dollars for expenses, IR scanners, a surveillance scope, a sniper rifle, communication gear, GPS locators, listening devices of all sizes and a mini surveillance camera and monitor. These kits were loaded.

Mack said, "Let's turn on the television; it is about time for the news. Let's see if there is any report of the break in at the warehouse."

We found a channel out of Dallas and listened to the broadcast. Nothing was said about the break in. This didn't mean that the guards had not detected the briefcases missing, just that they didn't report the information to the local news.

For three days and nights we watched for a team to show up with no activity. We were growing weary of waiting the impending attack and taking turns with guard duty. We were using the communication devices to listen for any traffic on the air. The only communication we received was an oilfield survey crew talking on their Motorola radios and an occasional dispatch from the local sheriff's office. Inside the lobby of the hotel we were able to stash a couple bugs and we set a camera up at the front door of the motel to view the faces of everyone that rented a room. The main problem we faced was we had to let the other team strike first, to ensure they were after us.

That night as we were preparing to trade shifts an SUV pulled into the motel lobby parking. It was a four-man crew; Mack motioned for me to look at the parking lot and asked, "Is that the team?"

I replied, "They sure fit the description of a team. I will watch them while you slip down and let Jim know that the team has arrived."

"Do you want us to stay in the room or come back up here to the surveillance area," Mack inquired?

"If you hurry you can come back here, but if the men get back into the SUV before you can get out of sight, head to the field behind the motel."

Mack left and within a few minutes he and Jim had joined me at our observation point. We could see the front door of our motel room and were protected by the motel roof from any rifle fire. We watched as two of the team members assembled their rifles and began surveying the area for a cover point. The final two members returned to the SUV and drove to a parking spot close to the front of our room. As one of the sniper team reached his position the radio traffic began. The spotter replied that he too was in position. We knew then that this was an assault team and that we were going to have to take them out. Mack focused in on the sniper and Jim took the spotter. That left the leads for me to take out. One of the leads moved up to the front of our room while the other covered him from the backside of the SUV. I knew our timing had to be on or we would miss our opportunity to take this team by surprise. Mack looked at me, smiled and said, "I rigged the door."

I knew what he meant but the explosion might rock the whole building and we were counting on surprise being on our side. If we missed our shots it would give the others a chance to lock in on our position. I whispered, "Find your target and fire as soon as you hear the explosion."

Seconds later Mack's trap was sprung, one of the leads kicked in the door. The explosion was loud, Mack and Jim fired before I did. Our targets were down. As quickly as possible Mack and Jim broke down their rifles and returned them to their briefcases. I put away my pistol and hurried to the ground. I jumped into the pickup and drove to the lobby. I went inside and told the cashier that someone had set off an explosive outside our room. As the cashier went to the phone to notify the police I gathered the bugs and the camera and returned for Mack and Jim.

Jim reached the truck first. He didn't wait for me to go back after him; he was coming across the parking lot towards the truck. I unlocked the passenger side door and he threw his case in the back and buckled himself into the seat. Mack waited for me to drive back for him. When we pulled alongside he jumped into the backseat and said, "Let's hit the road."

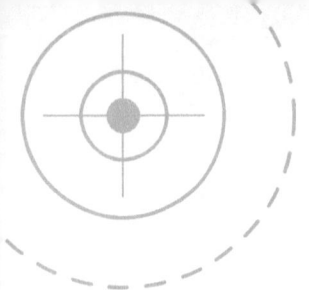

CHAPTER 12

OBTAINING THE LIST

We spent the rest of the day driving, after driving through half of New Mexico we turned north and headed towards Colorado. Colorado is not the right state to take on a team. The avenues of escape are slim pickings. I knew that a team would not expect us to head into Colorado so we did. We stopped that night in the town of Ouray. A quiet little town with a Swiss setting, the houses lined the slopes of the mountain range and the town was in the valley.

That night after we checked into a motel we received a phone call from John Clarkston. He said the President had contacted him and that the CIA had completed a list of the renegade members. We were to pick the list up from a post office box of our choice. I told John to have it sent over night to Gunnison, Colorado. I told him we would be able to pick it up in two to three days. This allowed us the opportunity to track another team and eliminate them. John also stated that my money for the story would be deposited into an account in a Swiss bank. When our conversation was complete John asked to speak with Jim. Jim took the phone and left the room. He was gone for about ten minutes and when he returned he was drinking a soft drink.

Mack asked, "What was that all about?"

Jim replied, "He wanted to know if we were having any problem protecting Chris."

Mack said, "Did you tell John that Chris could take care of himself"?

"No, I told him it took every waking moment to make sure he stayed safe but a good bonus would make up for our efforts."

I said, "I guess you guys should have a bonus, you have been living off of my money every since we left New York."

The next morning we were up early and headed out for Gunnison. We stopped in Montrose and had breakfast. It was around ten o'clock by the time we reached Gunnison, after a few minutes in a convenience store getting directions to the post office we were on our way. At the post office I went in and showed my identification and asked for the contents of my mail drop box. I was delivered an envelope and a package. I knew the list of agents was inside the envelope but I had no idea about the package. When I got back to the truck I slid into the passenger seat and instructed Mack to drive east. Our next destination was Colorado Springs. I knew an old buddy of mine from the agency lived there.

We had been on the road for about ten minutes when the contents of the package had Jim half out of his mind with curiosity, he said, "OK already, open the package!"

I looked into the backseat and asked, "Were you expecting a package?"

Jim said, "No, but since we received one don't you think we should open it."

I examined the packaging to see if I could detect any tampering and checked the address, the handwriting and the postage marks. They all matched, but I was not going to open the package until I had some idea of its contents. I flipped the cellular phone into the backseat and said, "Give John a call. Find out if he sent the package, if he didn't and you still want to open the package, we will let you out with it and you can open it."

Jim picked up the phone and dialed the newspaper. I could tell when John answered that he had sent the package by Jim's reaction. Instead of waiting on him to tell me what was inside I opened it myself. Inside the package was a bank deposit book for a Swiss bank and three envelopes, one for each of us. I slid Mack's envelope across the seat towards him and stuck Jim's and mine inside my jacket pocket. When Jim got off the phone he was grinning from ear to ear and said, "Go ahead and open the package, there is a little something in there for me."

I acted as though I was opening the package and when I felt enough time had been spent opening the box I raised my deposit book and asked, "What was supposed to be in the box for you?"

Jim leaned into the front seat and looked at the empty box beside my leg and said, "There were suppose to be envelopes with our names on them with expense money inside."

I reached into my jacket and pulled the envelope with Jim's name on it and asked, "Is this the envelope you were talking about?"

Jim snatched the envelope from my hand and ripped it open and said, "Why would you want to mess with me like that?"

I replied, "Settle down Jim, I was just passing time."

I opened the large envelope with the list of agents. It was a smaller list than I had anticipated. There were only twenty-seven agents names listed. I was not sure if this list was current or if we could cross six names off the list. I scanned the list for Mark Dillingham's name he was not present. I then looked at the list of agents that were no longer alive and his name was not on that list either. I began to read the remaining pages of the report and found that the hit list was also included. My name sat on the top of the list and two names below mine on the list was Mark Dillingham. Mark was a top agent during the eighties. We worked several larger drug busts together. In the mid eighties he was accused of taking the buy money for a large drug shipment. The money was marked by the CNA and even though Mark was accused of taking the money none of the marked bills had ever shown up.

We had been driving about three hours and I told Mack that the next opportunity to stop would be a good idea. Mack grinned and said, "It must be tough to get old."

I replied, "Beats the alternative."

Jim chuckled and said, "Mack he got you on that one."

I told the guys, now that we had the list of names we could start tracking the team members rather than waiting on them to hunt us down. I also told them we were going to Colorado Springs to pick up some help. Jim was resistant to adding a forth team member until I explained Mark's qualifications. As we neared the city limits of Colorado Springs Jim said, "Get your earpiece and put it on, there is a team operating in the area."

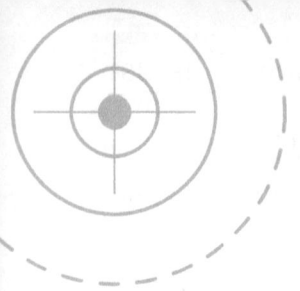

CHAPTER 13

A NEW MEMBER

I grabbed my earpiece and put it on. The conversation was definitely a team moving into position. I turned to Mack and said, "We need to get to the east side of town as quickly as possible."

Mack pressed the accelerator to the floor and we went speeding through the edge of town. I said, "Turn on North Hampton drive and head towards the zoo."

Mack glanced at me and said, "The zoo, I don't know where the zoo is! I'm from New York, not Colorado."

I said, "Follow the signs."

Mack made a hard right and then had to hit the brakes hard, as there was a big curve in the road. At the top of the road we were on was a black SUV parked on the corner with government tags. I told Mack, "Drive passed to the next street and we will walk back."

We pulled to the next street over and unloaded quickly from the pick-up. We grabbed our briefcases and headed across the front yard of a house in the neighborhood. When we reached the backyard fence I looked over to make sure there wasn't a dog in the yard. We opened the gate and ran through the yard to the back fence we climbed over into the alleyway. I was so worried about getting to Mark's house in time to save him that I didn't notice the operative in the alley. He turned towards me with his pistol drawn; I didn't have time to get to my 9mm and decided to roll. Just as I hit the ground I heard the gun shot. I anticipated the impact and waited for the burn, but I felt nothing. When I got to my feet I had pulled my 9mm and was ready to return fire. The operative was down. I looked back towards the fence I had just jumped over, with gun still smoking Jim said, "You said I would only last ten minutes with one of these operatives. I guess you underestimated me."

Still shaken from the idea of impending dome I smiled and said, "Thanks, but there are still three more of them out here."

I covered while Mack and Jim climbed the fence. When we were all in the alley I told Mack to get his rifle and see if he could climb onto a nearby roof. His hands were as fast as a cat's, he assembled his rifle and slid over the next fence and disappeared from sight. I moved up to where the operative Jim had shot was lying and told Jim that over this fence was Mark's house. We covered each other as we climbed over the back fence and hurried to cover by the back of the house. I kicked the back door open and rolled into the kitchen floor. Jim had my back. When I got back to my feet I felt the barrel of a pistol press firmly into my neck then I heard his voice. "You must be crazy thinking you can break into my house and take me out after all the time we spent working together."

That voice was unmistakable, even after all these years. I replied, "Mark, we are not here to harm you we are here to help you."

Mark pressed his pistol firmer into my neck and said, "We, you didn't come alone?"

I replied, "No, I am here with a couple of newspaper security men."

I never anticipated Mark would think that this answer was remotely funny, but he did. I could feel his hand begin to shake as he broke into laughter it was short lived. He immediately instructed, "Have them come in!"

I called to Jim and said, "Jim, I am with Mark, lower your weapon and come in."

I wasn't sure how Jim was going to react to this request; surprisingly he entered the room with weapon lowered. Mark then insisted, "You said you were with two men, where is the other?"

I answered, "He is on a roof with a snipers rifle, I am not sure where."

Just then my earpiece came alive with chatter; the team was trying to get the fallen operative to respond. I told Mark, "Take my earpiece and listen for yourself, there is a team here for you."

Mark complied, took my earpiece and listened. Finally he said, "How do I know you are not part of the team?"

Without thinking I turned to face Mark and said, "At my age! Jim killed one of the operatives in your alley if you want to chance going out to take a look."

It was the first time I had realized I was getting too old for this type of lifestyle. Before we could get Mark to trust us any further the front door was kicked open. Mark rolled to the hallway and I went through the other dining room. It was one of the leads, before I could get through the dining room into the living room I heard the sound of a pistol being fired through a silencer. I reached the living room just in time to take a shot at the intruder before he reached the hallway. I wasn't sure if I had hit him or not. I moved slowly through the living room staying down so as not be seen through the window. I assumed the sniper was watching me through an inferred scope. I positioned myself so I could see down the hallway and just around the corner were the soles of someone's shoes. Careful to not get shot by Mark I called out, "Mark, I have one down in the hallway, Jim will stay here in the dining room and monitor the front door, and I am coming back into the kitchen to watch the back door."

Mark did not respond. I moved back into the dining room and hurried back into the kitchen; I sat down behind the island and waited. Mark came around the corner from the hallway and said, "Are you hit?"

"No, are you?"

Mark replied, "You would be if I was! Now what is going on here?"

I slid away from the door opening a little more and said, "It is a long story, but the short version is, our old unit has gone renegade, anyone not choosing to be corrupt with them are being eliminated."

"So why are you here then, if not to eliminate me," Mark inquired?

"We came here to warn you and to try and get your help in hunting these guys down."

Mark was going to ask another question when the sound of a sniper rifle echoed within the house. Mark and I looked at each other and gave each other the thumbs up, I called to Jim, "Jim are you alright?"

Jim replied, "I am fine, do you need my help?"

I replied, "No, Mark and I can hold the back of the house."

I turned to Mark and asked, "What do you hear on the earpiece?"

Mark replied, "The leads are not responding and now the sniper is not responding either."

I said, "Mack."

Mark looked puzzled at my one word answer. I replied, "Mack is the other newspaper security agent that is helping us. We don't have time to spend talking we have to get to their SUV before the spotter gets away."

I called Jim and told him that we had to get the spotter; he and I ran from the house and climbed the fences on our way back to the pick-up. We reached the end of the street in the pick-up when we saw the SUV speeding away. Mack fired at the SUV but only hit the backseat window. As we prepared to give chase the SUV exploded and erupted into flames. I drove around to the front of Mark's house and he was standing in front of his house with a spent tank killer. I said, "You did that to the SUV?"

Mark replied, "I wasn't sure that this thing would even work. I kept it as a souvenir from my last mission."

I stepped out of the pick-up; Mark was still apprehensive as to why we were there. I told him to get in and we would explain everything on the way. Mark wanted to go back to his house and secure the doors and get a few personal effects before we left. I explained we didn't have the time. The police were going to be there any minute and we couldn't afford the time that would be wasted answering all the questions the police would have.

Mack came running up to the pick-up and was holding three wallets. I said, "Mack have you taken up looting?"

Mack replied, "No, I thought since you had the list identifying our targets, we could check and see where these guys are on the list."

"That was good thinking but we have an IR scanner that will read the barcode on their driver's license."

I introduced Mack to Mark, I said, "Mack Murphy meet Mark Dillingham."

Looking at Mark I added, "You have already met Jim Stephens; he was at your house helping us."

I began to explain about the organization going renegade and explained to Mark about the list. Mark relaxed a little and began to trust us. After several minutes had passed the police began to show up. Mark was able to lead us out of the area on little used back roads.

We had been driving for a while when Mark says, "You interrupted my lunch, do you think we could stop and get something to eat?"

Jim remarked, "Oh great another old timer that has to eat three meals a day."

Mark looked at me and asked, "Why is it that you are with these pups?"

"It's a long story, but the short version is I sold some pictures to their newspaper, pictures of a shooter. The shooter turned out to be from the agency and I was his target. I didn't realize at the time I was taking the pictures that I could possibly be the target. After I got to the newspaper, the editor assigned these two guys as bodyguards for me. They have proven their worth; we have eliminated three teams now and broken into the agency warehouse to get four briefcases for this mission."

Mark asked, "Who appointed you as the savior?"

"The President asked me to eliminate all the renegades from our old organization."

Mark looked defensive and asked, "Is that why you came to my house to eliminate me?"

I replied, "No, I came to ask for your help. We are good, but we haven't faced any real professionals yet. The guys we have been facing are working strictly from the manual. This makes them very predictable."

Mack interrupted, "We don't need this guy, if he doesn't want to be with us, let's drop him off and get on with the mission."

"Mack, don't blame Mark for having questions, don't you remember how unsure I was at the cabin of you two. We will just have to prove ourselves again and I am sure we will be able to handle whatever the agency can throw at us."

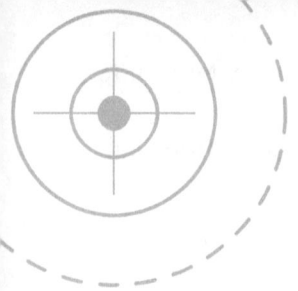

CHAPTER 14

SELECTIVE HUNTING

Not much more was said until we reached Trinity, Colorado. We stopped and fueled the truck and had supper. We planned on driving into Kansas before we stopped for the night. The address of one of the operatives was in Salina, Kansas.

Later that evening we pulled into a motel in Kansas. It was not a large town and there was only one motel. We rented two rooms and decided to get cleaned up and meet in my room to discuss the agenda for the following day. Mark and I were to sleep in one room and Mack and Jim the other.

I loaned Mark some clothes to wear and told him I would run to the store and get him a toothbrush and a few other necessities. I pulled out of the parking lot of the motel and headed towards town. There was an all night store open on the service road of the interstate. I went in and purchased the things Mark would need and headed back for the motel.

When I got back to my room Jim and Mack were already there. Jim snapped, "If you are going anywhere you need to let Mack or me know."

I smiled and said, "I have been taking care of myself for forty-eight years and don't think I need a babysitter now."

Mark chuckled and said, "Did you get our Gerital and vitamins?"

I replied, "They only had Centrum Silver, but I did get you Gresham Formula to wash that gray away."

Mack said, "You two think this whole thing is a big joke. I don't like the idea of getting up every morning and risking my life just to help you get your money."

"Money, what money? Who is paying for these hits," Mark insisted?

"No one is paying for the hits. The money is for the pictures I took and sold to the newspaper. We are on this mission at the request of the President. I am going to take a shower and get cleaned up."

When I got finished in the bathroom, I went back into the bedroom and Mack and Jim were going through the wallets of the three men from the Colorado Springs team. I said, "You shouldn't look at anything besides the identification cards. It is a haunting feeling to review the life of one of your victims. It adds a bit of humanity to them and in our business, you have to remain focused on the fact that they are an enemy and nothing else. If you try to put a name and a face on them then the job becomes increasing harder to complete. Where is Mark?"

Jim replied, "He walked out of here right after you started your shower. He said he needed to get some fresh air."

I scolded," Neither of you went with him, what were you thinking?"

Mack exclaimed, "Our job is to make sure you stay safe, Mark is not our responsibility!"

"He is a team member and should be treated as an important part of this team. He has skills that we need."

With that being said, I turned and headed out the door to look for Mark. It wasn't long into the search when I saw him on the corner of the motel using a payphone. I moved close enough to overhear the conversation; he was trying to convince someone to board up his house to prevent looting. As he hung up the phone I moved in and asked, "Did you use a credit card for that call?"

Mark replied, "Of course I used a credit card."

"Mark, we have to remain stealth, we can't leave paper trails."

Mark's lips tightened into a semi pout and then he said, "I'm sorry Chris; I have been out of the game for quite some time now. I still think

I can perform my part but I am afraid there are a lot of things that needs to be worked on. Remember I stopped receiving training drills when the agency dropped me for suspicion of theft."

I had forgotten that so many years had passed since Mark was a top agent. I knew he still had the heart for the job but was afraid he may have lost his edge. I responded, "Hey Mark, it is alright. It is not like you have had time to be briefed on everything that has happened. I know you didn't exactly come to us fresh out of the academy. As far as the agency's decision to drop you from the team, I knew you never took the money."

"Thanks Chris, it was hard adapting to civilian life with the stigma of being a thief hanging over my head. I instantly lost all of my old friends and had a hard time trying to make new ones. It is different making friends when you don't choose your friends based on trusting them with your life."

"I know what you mean Mark, now let's get back to the room so we can plan out tomorrow."

Back at the room, we began to plan how we were going to eliminate the agent in Salina. We decided we would stake out his residence and catch him when he exited the house. I also cautioned the team to remember not to leave a paper trail and to wipe down their room in the morning. Jim pulled the list out which had three names crossed off and had hand written a note at the bottom of the list that read:

Number of agents eliminated. 3 CONFIRMED, 7 UNKNOWN, 17 REMAINING.

The next morning we were on the road again by eight o'clock. It was an extremely cool morning and Jim volunteered to drive first. We hadn't been on the road for more than an hour when I received a phone call from John Clarkston. He said that he had received a call from the President stating that we could expect some help soon from the Bureau. This was good news for everyone in the vehicle, I think especially for Mack. I was not sure Mack had the stomach for this line of work. It is hard to do this job if you can't clear your mind of right from wrong. I believe Mack has a strong sense of justice and that is what allows him to continue with a mission that goes against his values. Jim and Mark on the other hand both appear to be able to perform their task with little thought of their deeds after the fact. I group myself with Mack, I have lost the desire to fix the world and find it more and more difficult to play judge, jury and prosecutor.

We pulled into Salina, Kansas around noon and decided to get something to eat before we tracked down the house that the operative lived in. We pulled into a burger joint and pulled out the map of the city. After several minutes of looking we found that 210 West Otis Avenue was about ten minutes away off of North 9th Street.

We pulled onto 9th street and found West Otis Avenue easily; we pulled off the street about a block from his house. A car was parked in the drive way and Mark decided we should go and check out the plates. When I told Jim and Mack our plans Mack said, "Perhaps Jim or I should go instead of you guys. We will be able to walk on the opposite side of the street and still be able to read the license plate."

Mark glared at Mack for a moment and then responded, "At least he thinks we are young enough to remember the plate number."

Mack responded, "Actually that was the next thing I was going to say."

Mark and I headed down the street towards the house, when we were across from the driveway I asked Mark, "Can you make out the tag number?"

Mark replied, "No, I was hoping you could."

We continued passed the house to the end of the block and crossed the street. As we were heading back towards the pick-up the front door to the house opened. A young man exited the house and was walking towards the car. This was a terrible time for us not to be in the pick-up. One of the first things you are taught on a stake out is never separate yourself from your vehicle. Too late for remembering rules, we had to decide whether to take this man or just follow him. While I was debating on which course to follow Mark spoke to the young man, "Freeze, we are federal marshals and we would like to ask you a few questions."

Great, I don't want to ask any questions, I want to eliminate this agent and move on to the next. The young man stopped in his tracks and asked, "Can I see some form of identification?"

I reached for my identification and badge and replied, "The name is Marshal Sloan, is this your house?"

The young man without hesitation replied, "Yes, it is my house, what business is that of the federal marshals' office?"

When I put away my identification, I pulled my pistol, fired one shot and replied, "None."

This was part of the reason I chose to retire; I lost the stomach for this type of work. I don't mind shooting someone that is trying to shoot me, but when you have to shoot someone face to face and your life is not in immediate danger it becomes much harder of a task. Mark bent down and found the man's wallet and looked at his driver's license. The name on the license was one of the men on the list.

On the way back to the truck Mark said, "I guess we can reduce the final count to 16 remaining."

I nodded and tried to remain focused on the facts, I had to keep reminding myself that this job must be completed. Mack had exited the pick-up and was walking towards us with a concerned look on his face. He asked, "Was that one of the guys we were after?"

I understood Mack's concerns, I replied, "Yes he was one of the guys."

We got back to the truck and I pulled the list from my case and crossed off the name. The next name on the list was in Lincoln, Nebraska. I told Jim, let's head for Nebraska. Jim started the truck and without any comment headed for the highway. I guess he knew I did what had to be done and was in no mood to talk about it. These last sixteen guys were going to know we are on our way to hunt them down and they will not be such easy targets.

CHAPTER 15

WARREN CONNECTION

We were only on the road for about an hour when the phone rang. It was John Clarkston checking in on us. I said, "We are down to only sixteen names remaining on the list."

He replied, "You can take an additional four names from the list, the bureau has them in custody and is questioning them now."

I asked, "How do you know this?"

John replied, "It is my business to know these things, I am in the news business."

Then he admitted, "The President called me earlier today with the news and asked for an update on your progress and he inquired whether you needed any additional men or supplies. The President went on to comment that the breech of the warehouse has been quieted and commends you on your ability to improvise for supplies."

"It was a team effort and a team plan that was executed flawlessly which allowed the operation to work so successfully. I just want you to know right now that without Jim and Mack I would have already been pushing up daisies."

John took a breath and said, "About Jim and Mack, this type of operation is not exactly why they were assigned to you. They were sent to hide you out and keep you safe, not to team up with you as aides to an assassin."

"So John, are you saying that you want them to return to New York?"

John replied, "I am not sure I want to abandon you, but I also don't want their death on my hands in case something were to go wrong with your plans."

I sat speechless for a moment then turned to Jim and said; "Pull off the road as soon as you can."

Jim pulled off the highway and asked, "What is going on?"

I handed him the phone and looked over at Mark and said, "Let's get some air and have a smoke."

We left the truck to allow Jim and Mack to have a private conversation with John. The last thing in the world that I wanted to do was accept the responsibility for Jim or Mack's life.

Mark lit a cigarette and asked, "Care for one?"

I took one from him and he lit it. He looked over at me and replied, "Just like old times."

I answered, "Not exactly like old times. In the old times we only had one or two targets and they weren't expecting us."

Mark said, "I don't mean the assignment, I mean you and I working together as a team again. It has a good feel to be back in the business."

I looked at Mark and said, "I never suspected you for taking the money in the first place."

Mark looked at me with a puzzled look on his face and asked, "Why not, I took it?"

Confused by Mark's sudden admission of guilt I replied, "I don't believe it, you were the most honest guy I ever knew."

Mark smiled and said, "Thanks for that vote of confidence; I was just wishing out loud anyway. I never took that money but I think I know who did. Paul Warren was the only member of the team left alone with the money and the only member of the team that stayed with the bureau after the rest of us retired."

"Now everything is starting to make since. You were a target because you were a threat to Paul Warren. I was a target because of a chance meeting with Paul in New York about a month before all this trouble broke out."

"What do you mean a chance meeting," Mark inquired?

"I was at a gallery opening and heard a voice call my name, I turned and looked it was Paul Warren. He asked whether I was still in the business or not. I told him I had been retired since the early nineties and had no desire to get back into the business. We spoke a few pleasantries and after exchanging or current business status we also exchanged addresses. I am sure that is where I made my mistake."

"So explain to me what mistake you are talking about, Mark said."

"I forgot you weren't in on the beginning of this whole thing, let me start from the beginning and bring you up to speed. I was in my apartment about a week ago and somebody starting shooting at my apartment building. At first I believed it was a random shooting and I got my camera and took some pictures. I took pictures of the shooter and the men that shot the shooter. I used two separate rolls of film and turned one in to the police and the other into the newspaper. John Clarkston, editor of the paper decided I needed to be hidden, that is where Mack and Jim come in. We were attacked at our safe house and have been hunting down the old organization every since. I tried to tell you this when we came to your house, but it was a little busy there. Besides we saved your life."

"That of course is assuming that I couldn't have taken care of myself," Mark inquired?

"Well we helped you take care of yourself," I insisted.

Mark looked as though he were going to comment and allowed the conversation to end without a word.

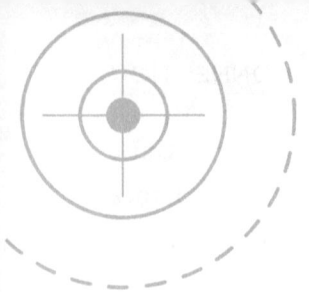

CHAPTER 16

EVADING THE NET

Mack came walking back to where Mark and I were talking and said, "We have a mission to complete, let's get to it!"

I looked up at Mack and asked, "Are you sure you want to continue with this?"

"It is the job we signed up for," Mack insisted.

We all got back into the pickup and I looked into the driver's seat and asked, "Jim, are you sure you know what you are getting yourself into? You don't have to help with this you know."

Jim hung an eye into the rearview mirror, grinned and said, "I can't leave this job up to you old timers, how do you think I would feel if I wasn't there for you when you flopped over a fence in front of an assassin?"

Without another word the truck started and we were back on the road headed for Nebraska.

As we neared Lincoln, I had a feeling that something wasn't right. I looked over at Mark and his face was scrunched in deep thought. I asked, "What's on your mind, Mark?"

He replied, "We are setting a pattern that would be easy to figure out."

I said, "I was just thinking the same thing. If they haven't already figured out that we have a list, they will shortly."

Mack turned around and asked, "What are you guys talking about?" Mark replied, "Survival!"

I added, "The men we are after are professional assassins. They live because they out think their advisory. I am not sure following the list and going to the nearest home is the correct plan. It leaves a way for the men we are after to trap us."

Mack nodded and replied, "Then you think we should randomly select someone from the list and go after them."

"No, I replied, I think we should continue with our present plan. Get the assassin in Lincoln and work out the details for the new plan afterwards. We still have the advantage of recognition. The agents don't know what type of vehicle to look for, but they do know our pattern. So we are going to have to change our attack methods."

Jim announced, "We are pulling into the city limits of Lincoln, if we are going to do something other than walk up to the front door, confront the agent and eliminate him, we better do it now."

As we neared the neighborhood, I noticed a team was setting up on the perimeter. I told Jim to get us out of the area as quickly as possible. This would be a blood bath and I wasn't sure it was one we could win.

Mark replied, "So this is the thanks we get for trying to clean up a mess in society."

Mack turned to the back seat and asked, "Are we going to scrub this mission?"

I replied, "No way, we are going to finish this. The only difference is now we will need to determine if we have enough fire power and the right men for the job."

We drove to the outskirts of town; when we neared a country road I suggested, "Turn down this road for about a mile and pull over."

Jim did as he was asked. When we came to a stop I suggested, "Let's get out and stretch. The job we have in Lincoln is unlike any I have taken on in the past. Those guys are all professionals and well trained. I am working with one man that has been out of the business for twenty years, two kids and me. Until this ordeal started I thought I was as capable as ever. Now I realize too much time has passed and I am not on the top of my game. It was luck that kept me from being killed when we went to save Mark. I know we couldn't rely on luck for this job. There must be several teams assigned to eliminating us."

Jim interrupted, "Since the only way this is ever going to be over is to eliminate everyone on your list. Why don't we get started"?

I wasn't sure that this task was my responsibility anymore. I knew in the old days that an assignment that I drew was because some big time drug dealer had figured a way into government officials' pockets and would not be properly handled in the judicial system. But what was my duty here. I am to be responsible for the assassination of over twenty men and quite possibly get some of my team killed in the process. At what cost do I place on ridding the world a handful of terrorist.

"Let's reason this one out, if we want the upper hand in this operation we will have to figure their attack plan and counter it. The things we have in our favor are no one knows when we will show up and they don't know where we are or what we are driving. The things they do know is that we are working our way down a list and striking state by state. They also know we only leave a paper trail when we are trying to draw them in. I am sure by now they have our pictures and can recognize us by sight."

Mack replied, "Why don't we just snipe them off like we did at the motel?"

"We could probably get two or three of their snipers and possibly one or two of their spotters before they would be able to flake our position and pick us off one by one," I responded.

Jim suggested, "What would be wrong with taking out one or two of the spotters or snipers and then just driving off and taking our chances with finding the rest of the team?"

Mark replied, "We need to finish this job and finish it now. We will have to plan a way to get all the men pulled in at once."

I looked at Mark as he had taken up his I am in charge stance and asked, "What did you have in mind for pulling the team all together?"

Mark answered, "Well, we could send one of these two kids up to the front door as a sacrifice."

Mack smirked and looked over in Jim's direction and said, "Or we could roll on of these old guys down the street in a wheel chair and let him crash into one of their SUVs."

I injected, "We could spend the rest of the days joking back and forth or we could brainstorm an idea that might keep us alive until tomorrow."

With that being said we got back into the truck and began to plan. We had worked over several ideas without getting the favorable results we were trying to achieve when Mark replied, "Let's take a break and get some food."

"Yea, food sounds good to me," Mack retorted.

Jim added, "I think better on a full stomach myself!"

Reluctantly I agreed and we headed back into Lincoln to find a restaurant. As we neared a small café I cautioned, "Keep any plans working in their heads and don't mention them in the restaurant. The last thing we need is to be discussing our attack plan and be over heard by some hungry agents. When we finish our meal we will go and check into a motel room and work out our strategy there."

The meal in the café seemed like a scene from the last supper, we ate and drank and hardly spoke. Each of us deep was in thought to try and figure how four men could eliminate up to twelve men. I knew if I were alone on this mission that I might take a chance on locating one of the snipers and hope the spotter didn't catch my muzzle flash. We could wait until dark and use the night vision goggles to locate and eliminate one or two of the snipers. I just couldn't work out a plan that would gather all the agents into one area without guaranteeing at least one of us not making it out.

I was still engrossed in thought when the waitress arrived with the check. Jim said, "Chris, I mean Mike, do you want me to pay for the meal."

Without any thought at all I replied, "Sure Jim, if you don't mind."

On our way to the truck Mack put his big bear like paw on my shoulder and asked, "Chris are you alright?"

"Of course I am alright, why would you ask?"

Mack removed his hand and said, "You were acting as though no one else was around in the café and we were just concerned about you."

I smiled and replied, "I am fine, thank you for your concern."

But I wasn't fine. I finally realized somebody was going to die when we took on this team. There were more of them than we can control. Each of them highly trained assassins. As we pulled into the motel we rented a room on the ground floor. I was either getting paranoid or I was getting a sixth sense, in either case I felt uneasy about being grouped together in one room with only one exit. We all sat on the beds and began to write out plans for discussion. After about thirty minutes of planning Mack says," I think I have the plan. We can divide into two teams, one team can monitor the vehicles that the agents are using and when they leave for supplies we can catch them off guard and eliminate them. The other team can remain behind and monitor the other vehicles. We can tag team eliminate these guys until we have them down to a manageable number."

Mark said, "Mack, don't you think when the first group are eliminated that the others will know it and then they won't separate anymore, besides what guarantee do we have that our team will be able to eliminate the first group?"

Mack replied, "I was just trying to come up with a plan that would eliminate these guys in small groups."

Still disturbed by the idea of being this close to the last mission and unable to plan it to completion I said, "Hold on Mark, Mack's idea is a start. We would be able to cut the numbers against us down with limited opportunity for loss on our side."

Mark said, "I don't have the patients to sit on a stake out until someone makes the first move."

"I feel your frustrations, but I don't have any better ideas. Jim, you have been awful quite, do you have any ideas?"

Jim replied, "I was thinking why not call in some help. We could call in the local police or even the FBI.

We could make a 911 call and claim we spotted men on the roof of some houses in our neighborhood and fled the area until the police could get the terrorist."

Amazed at Jim's idea I flopped back on the bed and let the idea run through my head. This might just work; the police could smoke the team out. We could follow any of the vehicles, which escaped and continue our mission. A few minutes of silence passed when Mark said, "That is as sound of a plan as we could have come up with except, how are we going to follow any of the vehicles?"

Mack said, "We could buy a high powered pellet gun and I could sit at the end of the street and shoot a hole in each of the tail lights."

Immediately the room irrupted in laughter, all but Mack. Mack said, "Don't laugh, if we work this right we can follow these guys for ever until we decide to take them out."

The laughter stopped and all eyes were on Mack. I replied, "You can't be serious?"

Mack said, "As serious as a heart attack. I told you I was a marksman. Any time the lights are on the white light escaping from the pellet hole will be like a beacon. We won't have to follow them close to see the light either. It is how the agencies used to mark the cars they were following before GPS and bugs were invented."

Mark replied, "You are a treasure of knowledge aren't you Mack?"

Mack smiled and continued, "I studied the ways the CIA, FBI, and treasury department used to tag their marks. One of the other things they used to do was smear a small amount of female moth pheromone on the backs of their mark when they were trying to track him on foot. The agents would follow along at a safe distance back passing a male moth inside a match box from agent to agent."

Mark interrupted, "What good was a male moth inside a match box?"

Mack continued, "The male moth would be excited by the smell of the pheromone and as long as they were within one hundred feet of the mark the moth would flap its wings which would beat against the sides of the match box making a constant clicking sound. If the moth quit flapping the agent had fallen too far behind or the mark had turned and gone a different direction. This method of tracking was very successful."

Jim said, "I hate to interrupt the history of the spy game but can we get back to now. What are we going to do? Are we going to buy a toy gun and shoot out lights or call 911?"

I could tell that the team was getting restless and wanted to get back to the business at hand. I said, "Let's go find that pellet gun and after we have positioned ourselves into the area we will call 911. While the police are doing our light work we can shoot out the taillights. Remarkable as it sounds, I think Mack's plan will work out just fine. The only thing we need to do is decide when we are going to execute the plan."

Mark had already stretched out on one of the beds and lifted his head and said, "Let's hold off until morning, we can all use some good sleep. You never know when the next time we will be able to sleep in a bed."

Mack seemed to buy into the plan; he had already untied the laces on his shoes and was preparing to lie down on the bed. I looked over at Jim and suggested we go to the lobby and rent another room so we all would have a bed to ourselves. He agreed and we headed up to the lobby.

In the lobby the lady at the counter explained the only room that was available was on the third floor. We took the room and after the card for the door was prepared and we had paid for the room we headed back to the pickup to get our bags.

As we arrived into the parking lot there was a government issued SUV parked in the lot. *This is why I hate motel rooms. There is no back door to the room, if these guys are a team and have figured out we are here we will have to fight our way out.* I looked over at Jim; he had already seen the vehicle as well. He pulled out his Swiss army knife, selected his auger blade and walked to the rear of the SUV and poked a hole in the tail light assembly. Upon his return I said, "Way to go MacGyver!"

Jim smiled and said, "There is one vehicle we won't have to shoot with a BB gun."

In the room, Jim said, "Do you think they know we are here?"

I looked over at Jim and answered, "If they knew we were here they would have shot you when you tagged their SUV."

Jim considered my answer and said, "Then why do you think they are here?"

I replied, "They are probably here for the same reason we are, to get a good night's sleep. I am sure they are waiting on us to show up. Now get some sleep."

I lay awake thinking what if I was wrong and they do know we are here. What if they have already eliminated Mack and Mark? Maybe I should go down stairs and check on them. I debated what action to take when I remembered Mark would not be taken out so easily. I got up and took a quick glance out the window, then returned to bed and tried not to think any more about what might happen.

The following morning I woke up to the sound of the shower water running. I looked over to Jim's bed, he was already up and showering. I got up and stretched then looked out the window to see if the SUV was still in the parking lot. It was still there and so were three more just like it. I backed away from the window, threw on my pants and shirt and my pistol harness. Now at least I wasn't completely naked. As I was preparing to go down to the first floor and check on Mark and Mack, Jim said, "Where are you going?"

I responded, "There are four government SUVs in the parking lot. I don't know if it means anything or not, but I thought I better go down and check on Mark and Mack."

Jim insisted, "Wait for me to get ready and I will go with you."

While Jim was rushing to get dressed, I picked up my stuff and closed my suitcase. I sat the suitcase by the door; I figured it would look less conspicuous to anyone watching if we left the room with our luggage. As I was getting ready to leave the room, Jim picked up the phone. I could hear him asking the operator to ring room 138. The phone rang twice before Mark answered. I grabbed the phone from Jim and said, "You need to get out of the room as soon as possible."

Mark replied, "Settle down, we already saw the agents. They are in the restaurant right now eating breakfast and planning how to take us down. Mack is sitting next to their table listening and having breakfast. I was thinking I might join him."

"Absolutely not, we can't take a chance that they might recognize you," I instructed.

Mark laughed into the receiver and said, "Settle down, I was joking, we are both sitting right here waiting on you two to come down the stairs."

I waited as Jim made his final pass through of the motel room making sure he had gathered all his stuff. I was amazed that he began wiping down the room without even being asked too. When he completed everything but the light switch and the doorknob he nodded for me to leave. He quickly wiped down the light switch and then the inside and outside doorknob. I was proud of him for how easily he caught on to this line of work but chose not to say anything about it to him.

When we reached the first floor, Mark and Mack had already loaded the pickup with their luggage and motioned us over to the truck. We drove out without looking back at the SUVs. When we were clear of the parking lot Mack said, "How close was that?"

I said, "We had better go ahead and get the BB gun so we can shoot the lens caps of the rest of the SUVs."

Mark said, "That won't be necessary, I had enough time this morning when they got here to mark each truck. In addition to tagging the lens caps I also placed transmitters under the fenders on all of the trucks."

I instantly got angry. I replied, "Have you lost your mind? What if they had seen you?"

Mark's tone changed from his happy go lucky style of talk to a firmer voice and said, "Wait a minute darling, just because you saved my life doesn't give you the right to decide how I live it!"

I realized Mark was right but before I could say anything, Mack leaned forward to the front seat where Mark was sitting and said, "Why do you call him darling, we are the ones that spent the night together?"

After hearing this, just as Mack had planned we all laughed. We needed something to break the tension and Mack's little joke did the trick. I apologized to everyone for the way I acted and then recommended we find some place to get breakfast.

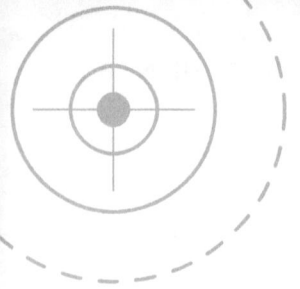

CHAPTER 17

THE 911 ASSIST

Shortly after we had completed breakfast the transmitters we had placed on the SUVs began to show movement. Mack was monitoring the movement on a small plasma screen display. When the vehicles stopped they were back in the neighborhood where our next hit was to take place. I decided it was time to call the local law enforcement. I dialed 911 on the phone; the operator asked what's the emergency. That is when I kicked into high gear, I replied, "There are some men climbing around on top of some houses and they have guns."

The operator enquired, "Are you calling from your house?"

"No, I got scarred and got in my car, drove out of the neighborhood and called 911 on my cell phone."

The operator then asked, "How many men?"

I replied, "At least 12 men, maybe even more. I am afraid they are terrorist or something like that!"

With that being said the operator asked me to hold on the line. I knew our plan was working; she would have to take this call serious. A few minutes passed and she returned to the line, "Are you still there?"

"Yes, have you sent the police?"

She replied, "The police have been dispatched to the neighborhood. I will need your name, phone number and home address for our records."

I decided the right thing to do was to give her the name and address of the man we were after. I said, "My name is Roger Jennings and I live at 215 Ross here in Lincoln."

The operator seemed convinced that the information she received would be sufficient for her report and allowed me to get off the phone. Mack asked, "Are we going to move in closer to watch the fireworks?"

I replied, "We should probably stay back so we can monitor the activity after the police are through with their investigation."

Mack said, "No, not the fireworks from the police. I was talking about the fireworks from the SUV; I placed one of my alarms on the back of one of the SUVs. When they open the back for their weapons, they will be history."

"You are a mad man. I can't believe you took the time to rig one of the vehicles with explosives."

Mack replied, "What time? They stick on and are armed; it takes less than ten seconds to attach one."

Mark interrupted, "What alarms and explosives are you guys talking about?"

"The explosives and alarms are the same thing. See when we were at the safe house and a motel in Baird, Texas, Mack rigged the doors with explosives. Both times the explosives served its purpose."

"So in a minute there could be an explosion," Mark enquired?

"Yep, and I don't think it will be long from now, the vehicles all appear to have stopped."

It wasn't much after this conversation that we heard the explosion. We weren't close enough to see the results of the explosion. As we neared the neighborhood police began flying into the area from all directions. I guess the 911 call worked, or maybe it was the placement of Mack's little surprise.

As we neared the area where the SUV had exploded we could already see that the firefighters were on the scene. Oddly none of the other teams had returned to their vehicles, because we were not tracking any movement on our monitor. The sound of sniper fire echoed through our pickup, Jim asked, "Should we get out and give the police a hand?"

Mark replied, "We didn't make helping a part of our original plan, I don't think we should go in there to help unless you plan on not returning."

I interrupted Mark before he could get going with his standard statement about a good plan is the only plan that works half the time. I said, "I agree with Mark, it would not help serve our purpose if we got involved now. We should stick to our plan and monitor the activity of the remaining teams. We will have plenty of opportunity to confront the survivors."

Jim pleaded, "What about the cops and their families, don't they deserve a chance to see their families again?"

I looked Jim in the eye and said, "It is not up to us to protect them, and they signed up for this type of work when they put their badge on their chest."

Jim insisted, "Yea I know that, but these guys they are fighting are professionals."

Mark replied, "Don't underestimate the police training, they are skilled and know how to deal with snipers."

Mack decided it was time for his two cents worth, he said, "I agree with both arguments, I just think if we kicked in to help we could turn the tide in favor of the police."

Before I could reply, Mark said, "Unless the police mistake us for snipers and then we will be targets for both sides."

Mack slipped on a pair of infrared goggles and began to systematically scan the area. He stated that there did not appear to be any rooftop snipers in position. As he continued to scan the neighborhood we heard additional small arms fire. Things were really starting to heat up. Mack noticed a small group of men slipping through a yard near the agent's vehicles and said, "They look like they are on the move."

Jim replied, "There is no activity on the monitor."

Jim backed the pickup into an alley and watched the monitor. Within seconds the vehicles began to move out. The agents came barreling passed us with two squad cars in hot pursuit. The squad cars were followed closely by what appeared to be an FBI vehicle. Jim said, "Shall we join in the chase?"

I replied, "Be patient, we have the monitor, there is no need for us to follow to closely behind."

Two more squad cars came ripping down the street, their sirens were blasting; I looked over at Mark and asked, "Do you think we have waited long enough?"

Mark replied, "I think we could wait a lifetime and it wouldn't be too long, but if we are going to get involved, we better get going."

Jim took Mark's response as a green light and sped down the street after the squad cars. I said, "Slow down Jim, the last thing we want to do is rush into some crossfire and catch a stray bullet."

CHAPTER 18

HUNT RESUMED

J im backed off the accelerator and we began to track the agents' progress on the monitor. The agents' vehicles headed for the interstate, much as we suspected they would do. At the interstate however, one vehicle headed North and the other South. Mack said, "They have split up, which group should we follow?"

I replied, "Let's head north, we have already been south."

At the interstate Jim took a right onto the interstate and Mack said, "We are about five miles behind the vehicle."

Mark smiled and said, "It's a great day to be alive."

He then looked over in my direction and asked, "Do you think maybe you can keep us this way?"

I answered, "I can't make any promises, but I think as long as we keep our heads we shouldn't have a hard time staying alive. After all the police are still between them and us."

We had been following the chase for about fifty minutes when we came pulling up to a roadblock. Jim rolled down his window and asked the officer, "Why we were stopped?"

The officer at first acted as though he didn't hear the question. Jim repeated, "We are Federal Marshal's and have a need to know."

The officer ventured over to our pick up and asked for identification. I flipped out my identification card and badge and asked, "Have you stopped the terrorist from Lincoln?"

The officer replied, "We have them blocked between us. We are holding the perimeter until the FBI can get here."

I was concerned that an advanced team of agents would also suspect they were being detained for the FBI or a SWAT unit and I knew they had no intentions of waiting for the big guns. I told the officer to have the roadblock opened and allow us to pass. The officer hesitated at my request and acted as though he was going to get on the radio for permission. I said, "I can't believe you are going to blow our cover!"

The officer turned to look at me and said, "I was just calling our commander for permission to let you pass."

I said, "I have already given you all the permission you need and I can't allow you to make any radio contact which might alert the terrorist that we are in the area."

The young officer was afraid of making any decisions on his own, so I aided him with his decision-making skills. I said, "Would it make it any easier on you if I had one of my deputies move the car for you?"

The young officer said, "No sir, I will be happy to let you through, just be careful."

Surprised at how easily people could be swayed just by viewing a badge I commented, "I should have had one of these years ago. I never realized how much power the sight of one little badge carried."

Mark looked over at me and said, "Don't you think we should have some form of a plan before we get ourselves in the middle of a hornets' nest with no way out?"

Impressed by Mark's desire to stay focused, I said, "What else is there for us to do other than drive up the highway and face whatever is ahead of us?"

Mark frowned and said, "I for one would like to be locked and loaded before we reach the agents. I also don't particularly like the idea of all being crowded together in one vehicle where we are sitting ducks if Jim gets hit."

Good point I thought to myself. Before I could express my views Mack added, "It would be nice to be in sniper range, without having to worry about a pistol taking me out."

Jim pulled to the side of the road after we had moved out of visual range of the roadblock and said, "Let's get our gear, we know we are going to need it so let's at least be that far ahead of the game."

We all got out of the truck and checked our weapons. I was thinking about Mack's statement that we should at least be out of pistol range. I said, "When you get ready to move up make sure we are in front of you."

Jim looked puzzled until I said, "We still need someone to stay with the truck in case we have to make a quick getaway."

Mark said, "So you expect us to walk the rest of the way?"

I looked at Mark and replied, "Unless you were planning on jogging!"

Those were our last words on the subject. I had made my plan, it was to stay back and hope their snipers weren't in position for a counter attack. Any other planning would have to be on the cuff. The days prior to this day were so filled with business that I literally didn't have time enough to catch my breath. I was looking forward to the end of this whole mess.

My thoughts were interrupted with the sound of high-powered weapons discharging. The trouble has started and we are still not in position to be a factor. I could tell by the sound that the agents were still several miles ahead of us. I signaled for everybody to pile into the back of the pickup and yelled in to Jim, "Take it easy, we don't want to get into range of their snipers without being able to defend ourselves."

As we approached the roadblock we could see that several police officers were already down and that the agent's vehicle had taken heavy damage. Mark and Mack slid out of the back of the trucks to take position on higher ground. Jim and I held back to assess the situation.

Without the advantage of communication devices we were all but cut off from Mack and Mark. Jim said, "It sure would be nice to know how many we are up against."

I looked at Jim, got out of the truck and pulled my infrared goggles out of the case and slipped them on. I scanned the area, there were two agents still in the SUV, one appeared to be hurt, he was slumped over in the backseat. The other was using the vehicle as armor. I spotted two additional warm spots working their way around the roadblock and one more agent that was lying in the street beside the vehicle. He also appeared to be hurt. I recapped my finding to Jim and he said, "Let's move in on the SUV and take out the guy that is running interference for the guys that are escaping."

I replied, "The police do not know if we are friend or foe, we might get ourselves shot trying to help."

Mack must have got in position, one high-powered blast rang out and the agent, which was holding the police at bay, collapsed onto the highway. Before I could stop him, Jim stormed off towards the SUV. I positioned myself to cover him as best I could. He ran up to the SUV, fired once at the man slummed in the backseat and slid through the front seat, opened the passenger side door and dispatched the other agent which was lying on the road. As quickly as it all began it was over, Jim raced back to the pickup with a grin from ear to ear. When he got within speaking range I said, "That was the most irresponsible action I have ever witnessed! You could have been killed."

Jim replied, "Let's surrender to the police so that we can get on with our assignment."

Flabbergasted by the entire display I realized there was a time in my life when I would have acted the same way. I smiled and said, "OK kid, you are making good sense now." I placed my pistol on the dash of the truck next to my goggles and stepped out of the pickup."

The police had already begun moving beyond their blockade and had moved up to the SUV. With my badge in hand, I raised my hands over my head and started walking towards the oncoming officers. Needless to say these guys were extra cautious when they approached us. The standard orders for arrest were barked in our direction. Kneel on the ground; keep your hands where we can see them. We complied and the next set of commands was barked in our direction. Lie down, face first on the ground, spread eagle position. Again we complied; as the officers stormed in on us they were a bit rough. I didn't blame them, several of their friends had already been killed and they were not taking any chances with us. As I lie face down on the ground I could hear the sound of ambulance siren coming up the road behind us. The officers placed cuffs on Jim and were in the process of cuffing me when one of them spotted the federal marshal badge. He asked, "Are you a federal marshal?"

I replied, "Yes I am, Marshal Sloan and that is one of my deputies. If we can complete this interrogation within the next few minutes, perhaps we will still be able to get the two men, which you allowed to slip through your roadblock."

The captain of the highway patrol stepped over to where I was being molested and said, "What are you talking about? There were only three men in the SUV when it pulled up in front of our roadblock."

I replied, "Then they must have known you were set up for the roadblock because I watched two men escaping through the hills, one on either side of the highway. Get these cuffs off of me and I will prove it to you."

The captain ordered my cuffs removed and he and several of his men escorted me back towards my pick up. To avoid any unnecessary conflict with the weapons in the vehicle I replied, "Have one of your men pull the vision goggles out of the front seat."

The captain said, "Miller, get those goggles."

The goggles were handed to the captain and he began to scan the hills near the roadside. I replied, "You should view four separate heat sources, two of those sources are my men, the other two are escaped terrorist from your roadblock."

The captain had surveyed the area and spotted three separate heat sources. He said, "I see three separate sources, but I can't locate the fourth."

I asked, "Is this enough proof to allow my deputy and me to assist my other deputies? After all these men are professional terrorist."

The captain was hesitant with his answer, "Finally he replied, I guess we will allow you to assist, but when this thing is over I expect a full report."

The captain turned back towards his men and ordered the release of Jim. As I started back towards the truck the captain sank my goggles gently into my midsection and said, "Remember you owe me a complete report."

I nodded acknowledgment in his direction and got into the truck. When Jim climbed into the passenger seat I told him to drive about two miles past the roadblock and pull over. I put on the infrared goggles and began to scan the countryside. I was able to locate Mack and the agent he was after, but I could not seem to spot Mark or the agent he was trailing. When I looked back to where I had last seen Mack I noticed he was crouched down on one knee. I looked over at Jim and said, "Pull over, Mack has found his shot."

Before I could finish my sentence we heard the echo of the round from Mack's rifle, I looked towards the last place I had seen the agent and saw his body laying on the ground. I handed Jim my goggles and instructed Jim to stay with the pickup. I headed up the side of the hill to where I had seen Mack last. When I got within hearing range Mack said, "I am not sure if he is hit or not, he went down at the same time I fired."

I replied, "Then you stay back and cover me and I will go in and check."

I wondered why I hadn't brought my goggles with me. I could scan the body without moving in. It was at that exact moment I remembered that Mack's rifle had infrared lens. I looked back in Mack's direction and asked, "Mack can't you scan the body for heat."

For a second Mack failed to respond then he said, "Sure I guess I could do that."

This was the second time that I had a feeling that I couldn't trust Mack. I wasn't sure why I kept feeling this way about him. He had proven himself to be reliable and dependable on several occasions, but I learned long years back, if you can't trust the guy you are working with you better get another partner. Mack said, "I have been watching him for about a minute and it appears his heat source is fading."

In our line of work, if the heat source is fading that means your target has expired. I asked, "Mind if I take a look?"

Mack replied, "Not at all, I would rather you felt comfortable before you move in to identify the guy."

Mack extended his rifle towards me. Looking through the scope I could clearly see after about a minute that indeed the temperature of the body was dropping.

As I approached the agent I pulled my 9mm just in case. I knelt down beside the agent and he said, "Are you Chris Moore?"

Instead of just answering him I rolled him over to face me, I removed his communication piece from his ear and pulled the transmitter out of his pocket. I found the on/off switch and silenced the device then I answered, "Yes I am."

He then asked, "Why have you turned on us?"

I replied, "I didn't turn on you, the agency has put a hit out on me."

The man's eyes rolled to the back of his head and then refocused on me and he said, "You have been deceived, someone is using you against us. You were to be taken into protective custody by us and a standing order was sent to take you alive that was until you eliminated the second team in Texas. An order was placed to have you eliminated at that time."

Surprised by the new information I began to wonder who or whom had put the original hit out on me or if that order was even issued. I asked, "Who tried to shoot me in my apartment?"

The agent reached out and grabbed my arm, struggling for life and said, "No orders were issued for you until you eliminated the team down in Texas. Now do something for me, get my wallet and make sure it gets delivered to my wife, my address is on my driver's license. Tell her."

That was everything the agent said until he expired. I was feeling betrayed, but I wasn't sure who had betrayed me. I spoke directly with the President; surely he wouldn't lie to me. I started replaying every conversation I had since the shooting started. I remember the offer to come in was issued, but that doesn't explain the man that was at my motel room door. Who all knew I was in that room? It should have only been Mr. Clarkston, his assistant and me. I know I never tipped anyone that I was there, unless I was followed the entire time. Ridiculous, I would have sensed if someone was tailing me.

I pulled out the IR scanner and flashed the agents ID chip to check him off the list. I pulled his wallet and placed it in my back pocket and began to retreat to the truck. I was half way down the hill when I heard the sound of a sniper rifle. I had forgotten all about Mark and the agent he was following. Mack shouted, "The shot came from around the bend in front of us."

He began to jog towards the position. I called after him and cautioned, "Don't forget to scope the area before moving in."

Rather than chase after Mack I chose to distance myself about three hundred yards behind him. The terrain was rough and some of the ground was loose from erosion, several times I almost lost my footing. I moved down the hill so the slope wasn't so great and began to pace myself with Mack. As we neared the bend I noticed Mack dropped to one knee and began to scope the area. He sat locked on one position for about two minutes, when I got close enough to talk without shouting I asked, "Is the agent down?"

MANHATTAN SHOOTING

Mack swung his head in my direction and replied, "Yes and he is losing heat fast."

I then asked, Is Mark alright?"

Mack had repositioned his rifle and nodded in response rather than answer. Several minutes passed before Mack lowered his rifle and then he said, "Let's get the IR scan of the body and get back on the road. I am exhausted."

I realized we have been pushing hard the past couple of weeks and we all could use a rest. We headed for the area where Mark was set up. As we neared the highway the captain of the highway patrol was waiting on us. I gave the IR scanner to Mack and said, "Go up to the agent and scan his identification and meet me back at the truck."

The captain motioned for me to come over to his car and asked, "Did your men get the two terrorist that escaped?"

I replied, "They did."

He asked, "Are your men both alright?"

"Yes, they are fine. We are doing an IR scan on the last terrorist for our report and we will be on our way back to D.C. to complete our paperwork and get a new assignment."

The captain looked rather confused and said, "Aren't you going after the others?"

Without letting the captain know that we were already aware of the other agents heading south I asked, "What others?"

He replied, "There was another SUV full of terrorist which headed south at the same time these guys entered the interstate. They were able to break through the road blocks and are probably on their way to Mexico by now."

I already knew these guys would break through any obstacles that were in front of them. Acting surprised at the thought that other agents were on the highway I asked, "Do you have surveillance on them or will I need to order a helicopter?"

The captain acting quite proud of himself and his men stated, "We do have them under surveillance and you can communicate with the helicopter pilot on this radio. Just remember to have it dropped back by my office when this is all over. The call number for the pilot is PN6700."

I took the radio and thanked the captain then joined Jim in the truck. Inside the truck I instructed Jim to drive up to where Mack and Mark were standing over the last agent. Mack and Mark watched as we approached and they began to journey down the side of the hill.

Mack swung open the door to the pick up and asked, "What about the others?"

I picked up the radio and showed it to Mack and said, "The captain of the highway patrol loaned us his radio to stay in contact with the helicopter pilot."

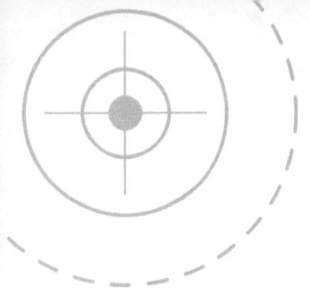

CHAPTER 19

HELICOPTER SUPPORT

When Mark got in the truck we drove to the nearest turn around and headed back south. When we passed the area where the two vehicles entered the interstate I picked up the radio and said, "This is US Marshal Sloan calling the pilot of PN6700, over."

The pilot replied, "This is PN6700, what can I do for you today Marshal?"

I replied, "PN6700, we would like to know the location of the terrorist which broke through the road block on the interstate, over."

The pilot replied, "The terrorist are below me and the radio you are talking on is only a two way radio. I have one of the radios and you have the other, so don't worry about trying to use call letters and ending each statement with over. If you want to contact me just pick up the radio and talk. If you feel you need a name to use to make the conversation easier you can call me Bob."

I replied, "Thanks Bob, how about the location of the terrorist."

Bob replied, "They are still beneath me and I am approximately twenty miles beyond where the terrorist broke through the road block."

I looked over at Jim and said, "Floor it; we have a lot of ground to make up."

HELICOPTER SUPPORT

Jim did as asked, we reached the area where the roadblock had been set up, and there were ambulances and other emergency units all along the highway. I waited until we had cleared the area where the agents' shot there way passed the roadblock and instructed Jim to tromp on the accelerator. We were flying down the highway; there was no traffic between the agents and us. We had been on the road for about 45 minutes when the radio sounded, "Marshal, this is Bob, I still have a visual on the terrorist they are approximately seventy miles from where they broke through the road block. The bad news is that I have been in the air as long as my fuel supply will allow. I am going to have to break off surveillance and return to base for refuel."

This news actually delighted me more than disappointed me, I knew when the agents saw the surveillance chopper break off for refueling that they would leave the interstate at the nearest possible exit. I replied, "Bob, if you could do one thing for us before you break away. Please check the nearest mile marker and let us know what it is."

Bob replied, "That will be no problem, the nearest mile marking is one eighteen. I will try and relocate these guys after I fuel up."

"Thanks for your help Bob; we are still about thirty miles behind you."

The information we didn't feed to Bob was that we really didn't need his help to track these guys. I looked over to Mack and said, "Turn on the monitor and let's track the missing agents."

Mack reached for the case the monitor was in and turns on the unit. After a few seconds the blip and the ping sound began to show up on the monitor. Mack said, "It looks like they are still on the interstate."

I replied, "Turn the volume down and let me know when they turn off the interstate."

Jim was pushing the pickup close to its maximum speed. We were flying down the highway at about hundred and ten miles an hour. I opened up the glove box and pulled out a half eaten roll of antacid and chewed up a couple pills. Jim noticed what I was doing and asked, "The pressure getting to you old man?"

I replied, "More like the spicy sausage that I had this morning for breakfast."

Mark interrupted, "That must be why my stomach thinks by throat is cut, it has been seven hours since I have eaten anything."

Mack reached into his jacket pocket and pulled out four individually wrapped blueberry muffins and simply replied, "Continental Breakfast."

I unwrapped Jim's muffin and handed it to him. Mark replied, "I don't guess you would have a pot of coffee in the other pocket would you Mack."

We chuckled and Mack replied, "Sorry I had to pour it out this morning when we took our hike in the hills."

Jim injected, "Just as well, if you would have left it in the truck this morning it would have been stolen by that overzealous captain of the highway patrol that decided we needed to be handcuffed."

Mack asked, "What handcuffs?"

"Oh, while you guys were out taking your morning stroll, Chris and I were thrown on the ground, cuffed and questioned," Jim replied.

Mark reentered the conversation by saying, "You don't have to tell me how you got out of the situation. I have worked with Chris too long. He used his new cover as Michael Sloan US Marshal and sweet-talked his way out of trouble. Am I right?"

Jim acted amazed by Mark's skillful discernment and said, "Yes you are right, that is exactly what happened. Were you watching from the hill?"

Mark replied, "Of course not, I was a little too busy following one of the agents to be concerned about Chris. He has always been able to take care of himself and any other member of his team that needed to be taken care of."

As pride began to swell up inside of me thinking that I was so well thought us by my fellow agents and just as I was going to reciprocate the complements back to Mark he continued, "Of course, Chris Moore AKA Michael Sloan has always had a gift for B.S."

As the laughter erupted inside the pickup and the red glow of embarrassment faded from my cheeks I was relieved that I didn't begin to complement Mark and cause the embarrassment to be any worse. Our lighthearted moment was short lived when Mack said, "It looks as though they are leaving the interstate and believe it or not there appears to be two vehicles."

I insisted, "How can that be? The helicopter pilot didn't report but one vehicle."

Mack replied, "I don't know how it can be but I definitely have two distinctive blips on the screen."

Looking into the backseat to catch a look at the monitor I confirmed there were two distinct beeps on the screen. Mark had pulled a map and noticed an adjacent road to the interstate. He said, "Looks like when we followed the group north that the two remaining vehicles headed south. One exited the interstate at the first off ramp and intercepted the adjacent highway to meet up later if there was any trouble. The reason we didn't see them on the screen at first was they were outside the range of the monitor.

I took a look at the map and replied, "That makes sense, I am sure we would have worked a plan similar to this if we were the assault team. Mark's idea about them being out of monitor range also makes sense."

We had closed the gap between assault team and us to under fifteen miles; we would be catching up to them pretty quick. Mack said, "How are we going to play this, two teams turns the odds in their favor?"

I agreed with Mack by saying, "Mack is right, we do need to decide what approach to take."

Mark said, "It seems as though we have been playing this whole mission by ear, do we actually need a plan. Why don't we just wait and see what opportunities present themselves?"

Jim said, "We need to decide on something pretty quick, we are closing in enough that we should have a visual within the next ten to fifteen minutes."

I wasn't sure how to proceed, I knew I could rely on Mark but I felt uneasy about trusting the other two. I wasn't sure if I was getting overly cautious in my old age or if my instincts for sniffing out a rat were working overtime. There are times when you don't show your entire hand at once and I had questions that needed answered but I didn't know where to get the answers I was looking for. I began to replay the events back to the beginning. Perhaps there was something I had missed. Then it dawned on me, it was the pictures, the pictures were what caused me to distrust these two. Until I could study the pictures a little closer I was going to keep these two out in front of me, so I could keep an eye on them. Mark asking, "What is the matter Chris", interrupted my thoughts?

I replied, "I was trying to decide what to do next. I think we should follow these guys until they stop for the night. We can assign a birddog to them and the rest of us can get some rest."

Jim replied, "Suits me, I could use some rest."

I looked back at Mack and said, "Mack, you better try and get some rest now, it looks like you will have the first watch."

Mack acknowledged my statement by nodded his head and offering the lap held monitor to me. I took the monitor and began to watch, as we were steadily closing in on the blips on the screen. Jim asked, "If we know where these teams are why couldn't we get the FBI or another government agency involved to take these guys out with a smart bomb or something?"

I replied, "The government doesn't work like that, they cannot afford to get involved in clean up missions like we are on. We are the government cleanup crew. The way we operate draws the least amount of public attention and the local law enforcement agencies are more than happy to cooperate on a need to know basis when they are informed that a government agency is involved."

We were nearing Salina Kansas when we exited the highway. The blips had come to rest somewhere within the city limits of Salina. I felt like perhaps they were at a motel or a restaurant. When their vehicles came into view we were shocked to see they had pulled up in front of the local police station. Mark growled, "What the heck are these guys up to?"

I wished I had an answer for him but I didn't have a clue. I pulled out the phone and pressed the speed dial number for John Clarkston, on the third ring he answered. "John I need your help, the agents we were following have pulled into the local police headquarters and we are not sure what they are doing there."

John replied, "I will get right on it, I have friends at Salina."

Not trying to let on that John had done anything wrong, I replied, "Thanks for your help and we will be awaiting your call."

When our good-byes were said, I immediately began to wonder how it was that John knew we were in Salina. I know none of us had told him. I have had the phone on my person for the last several days. We have not been apart as a team since this morning. Could it be that we are being set up and that John is perhaps behind the whole thing? Something must be done about this. I began to wonder what I had gotten myself into. I suggested, "Let's go find a motel and freshen up then try and get some rest. I feel like the agents were not going to travel again tonight."

Mark agreed by saying, "Sounds like a plan to me."

Jim pulled the pickup into the motel and went in and rented two rooms. When he returned with the swipe cards, I announced, "Let's get cleaned up and meet in the restaurant in an hour."

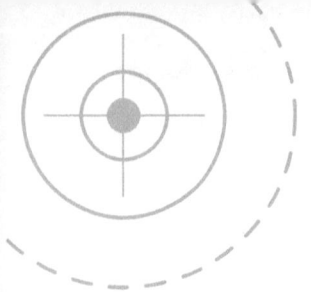

CHAPTER 20

THE BUG

When everyone had emptied the truck of their belongings and Mark and I were in our room I said, "Mark, I think we have a problem, John knew we were in Salina without me telling him."

Mark perked up and replied, "Do you think he has a GPS planted in your truck?"

"No, there was no way for John to know that I had bought this truck. It has to be something else."

Mark said, "Let's review anything that we received from John."

"First there was the phone which you have been using the entire time, the envelope of money, the package with the agents names identified. I can't think of anything else that John had his hands on prior to us receiving it."

Mark answered, "Let's go for a ride and we will get rid of everything that could hold a GPS transmitter. We can start by getting a new phone."

Mark and I got into the truck and began to drive off. As we were driving down the road Mark began to examine the envelopes which were placed inside my case. He exclaimed, "There is no way to bug any of this stuff, everything is too small."

While Mark was talking I remembered the pictures that Jim brought along at the beginning of the trip and the gun and luggage, which Jim had also provided me. I looked over at Mark and replied, "My luggage or my pistols, both were provided by John."

I slipped out of my harness and handed it over to Mark and said, "Check this thing out, I have had it on every since the safe house. I

have always been puzzled how the first group of agents found us at the safe house anyway."

As Mark inspected the harness for tracking devices he looked over at me and said, "Bingo."

After a few moments of prying the false cap off of one of the brads, which held the harness together, he removed a miniature GPS transmitter, which transmitted through the GPS system on my vehicle. Now there was an additional issue. If the GPS transmitter used my trucks GPS to transmit that meant my vehicle identification number was also known. I stopped the truck and said to Mark, "We have been tagged this whole time and the truck is not secure anymore either."

Mark appeared a bit confused and asked, "How is the truck not secure?"

I replied, "The transmitter you pulled from my harness was using the truck's GPS transmitter to send the signal, that means whoever is on the receiving end of the transmission also know our VIN number and can track our truck."

Mark reacting as though a light switch had been flipped on in his brain said, "Oh I get it, let's steal another truck."

"It's not that simple, we need something that can't be traced and that we won't have to swap out every day or so."

Mark said, "You got any ideas?"

"Of course I have ideas! The first thing we need to do is buy me a new shoulder harness, pistol and luggage. Then we go get a new truck and get back to the motel and re-evaluate who we can trust and who we can't trust."

Mark said, "Wal-Mart it is."

Upon arriving at the parking lot at the store I looked to Mark and asked, "Do you want to come in with me, this may take some time."

At first Mark didn't reply he was studying the pictures I had taken at the Moore Towers. He then responded, "I think I will wait here, next to the dentist office there is nothing more I hate than shopping."

I told Mark that I would hurry and headed for the store. In the store, I quickly grabbed a buggy and headed through the aisles locating the things I needed, clothes and toiletries. Anything that I didn't provide for myself had to go including the clothes I was wearing. I went to the register with a complete change of clothes and paid for them then went into the changing room and took off the clothes I was wearing. I pulled the contents from my pockets and as I was changing them over I remembered that the badge was not purchased by me. I decided I would go to the truck and get Mark.

I arrived at the truck and Mark was nowhere to be found. I wasn't sure what this meant, had he gotten bored and came in to look for me or had something happened to him. I couldn't waist time couldn't waist time looking for him now, I had a lot to accomplish and a short time to get it accomplished.

Back in the store I reunited with my buggy and headed for the guns, which were located in the back of the store. As I reached the counter I saw the pistol that I wanted and asked to see it, the balance was fine and this was the pistol I wanted, the problem was that this was a pistol and there is a ten-day waiting period to purchase a pistol in Kansas. Great I thought to myself, I would have to tear down the pistol I have and inspect it for bugs. I went ahead and purchased a new harness for my old pistol and told the guy at the counter I wasn't interested in the pistol.

On my way to the checkout line I remembered the phone. I went and found the electronics section and purchased two cellular phones and one thousand minutes. I didn't want to have to get another set of phones any time soon.

In the checkout line I noticed Mark over by the photo center in the store, he was pacing as though he was impatiently awaiting the birth of his first child. As the girl in the checkout line quoted my charges, I fumbled for the money and told her to keep the change. I grabbed the bags and pushed my buggy in the direction of Mark.

I asked, "Mark, what are you doing in here."

Mark smiled with a cat like coyness and replied, "I will let you know as soon as I find out.

Have you talked with the guys to let them know where we are?" "No, do you think I need to?"

"You told them we would meet in the restaurant in an hour, that was about fifty minutes ago. Did you get the new phones?"

"I completely forgot about the restaurant, I will call them right now and yes I did get new phones."

Mark replied, "Don't use one of the new phones, and call them on the old one."

I understood Mark's concern, "If the old phone was being monitored I might as well continue to play along as though nothing were wrong."

I called the guys and told them Mark and I had decided to go out for a bite to eat and they should go ahead and eat in the restaurant and we would see them in the morning. When I got off the phone with Mack and Jim, I turned back to Mark to find out what exactly he was up to. I asked, "So why are you acting so secretive?"

Mark replied, "That's an easy question, I am a secret agent."

Hearing this took my mind off of the trader in our midst and caused me to laugh. Mark was waiting for my reaction before he joined in on the jubilation. We were still laughing when the young girl at the counter of the photo center announced to Mark that his pictures were ready. He moved closer to the counter and she seemed as though she was apologizing for something then handed him the envelope that contained the pictures. I approached the counter as Mark was pulling his wallet to pay for the pictures. I replied, "I will pay for the pictures."

As I pushed my way up to the counter, Mark was pulling at the cover of the envelope to view the pictures inside. He removed the pictures as I was paying the cashier. Suddenly he said, "Oh my gosh, it is him. I suspected it was him before I blew up the pictures but I had to make sure."

I turned away from the counter and reached my hand for the pictures and Mark said, "Not here, I think we should be outside and away from everyone before you see."

I was as anxious as kid with a new toy, I could hardly stand having to wait to see the pictures. As I was hurrying out of the store the stupid sensor at the front door went off. I hate that Gestapo style these stores try to put you through. They want your receipt then they want to match it up to every item in your shopping cart and expect you to wait patiently as they pry through everything you just purchased. I explained to the lady that I was in a hurry and I assured her that I had not stolen a thing. This entire spiel fell on deaf ears, she continued to insist that I hand her the receipt and step back while she inspects my purchases. I started to pull out my badge and tell her she was under arrest for harassing a federal marshal put decided that this would only prolong my wait, so I complied.

After what seemed an eternity we reached the parking lot and Mark took over pushing the shopping cart towards the truck and handed me the pictures. He had noticed an image in one of the pictures I had taken in a mirror in the room and had that image enhanced. To my amazement and shock the image was Jim Stephens. What was Jim doing in the room where the shooter had been? Mark grew impatient for my response and said, "Well, what do you think Jim was doing in the room?"

I replied, "I don't know, I had not been to the paper yet, so unless Jim is tied in with the shooter I don't know what he was doing in the room."

Mark replied, "When we get back to the motel I will take him out."

"We can't just take him out without giving him a chance to explain why he was there."

Mark insisted, "Why not, it wouldn't be the first time we made a hit without giving someone a chance to explain?"

"We didn't know the guys we took out, but we did know they were an assigned target and it was a part of our job. With Jim it is different, he has been working with us the entire time and I have no reason to suspect that he would turn on us."

Mark replied, "I am sure that is what Hitter thought when Mussolini switched sides."

"Come on Mark, you know he saved my life when we came to rescue you."

Mark said, "Did he save your life or just prolong your life until he finishes his mission?"

"He saved my life and he has not caused me much reason to suspect him."

Mark asked, "Then there could be some suspension which you are not sharing with me?"

"There was the time when the first assault team arrived when we were still at the safe house when I felt as though there was going to be some problems. I remember he bird-dogged my every move. I also found it suspicious that the assault team was so quick to arrive on the scene at the safe house. The main issue with Jim that sticks in my mind was when the assault team was eliminated and I got the drop on Jim and Mack, I asked for their weapons. Mack was quick to comply but Jim was very hesitant, that still bothers me to this day. Why was he so hesitant to relinquish his weapon if he had nothing to hide?"

Mark responded, "I don't find the lack of willingness to relinquish his weapon suspicious, I would have a hard time giving up my weapon too. What I find to be suspicious is the fact that Jim provided you with a bugged harness and was at the original scene where the shooter was and has never attempted to explain his presence there. What was he doing there if it wasn't to put a bullet in your head?"

"Mark you have a strange way of putting things into perspective, but when you pose a question like that I feel as though I must somewhat agree with you."

"Then we have to take him out," Mark insisted.

I loaded my new belongings into the back seat of the pick up and walked around to the driver's side and got in. Mark slid into the passenger seat burning a hole through the side of my head with his eyes waiting on my reply. He didn't get one, I wasn't sure what to do and I didn't plan on thinking about it now. I started the truck and pulled out of the parking lot.

We had been driving for about ten minutes when I spotted a car dealership with the replacement truck I needed. It was a GMC extended cab with an oversized toolbox and didn't appear to be very old. I whipped into the lot and went straight for the front door of the used car dealership. As I reached for the door a man met me coming out. With his hand extended he introduced himself and asked what service he could provide. I replied, "That GMC out front is it in good shape?"

The dealer replied, "Of course it is in good condition, it has less than twenty six thousand miles and has never left the main road. It is a steal at thirty two thousand."

I replied, "It certainly would be a steal if I paid you thirty two thousand for it. I intend to buy that truck and I don't intend to pay more than twenty thousand for it."

The dealer chuckled for a second, then looked me in the eye and said, "Then you better keep looking, that truck caused me twenty four thousand this morning."

"I am sure you will find some poor sap to pass on your losses for this truck in the near future, but for now let's go into your office and get the keys and the paperwork done so that I can get out of here."

The dealer said, "My rock bottom price is twenty three thousand."

I chose not to respond to his offer and continued walking towards his office. At the door to his office I asked, "Does anyone else need to be talked to before we make this deal?"

The salesman tugged his pants up and said, "I don't think so, I am the owner of this dealership."

The dealer began to type out the contract and when he got to the place where the price should be entered he looked up from his keyboard and said, "We agreed on twenty three thousand, correct?"

I opened my brief case and pulled twenty thousand dollars and sat on top of his desk and replied, "Nope, we agreed on twenty thousand dollars and any argument from you this money goes back into the brief case and I head down the road to the next dealership."

The man looked over to the window to view the truck for one last time and said, "You are killing me here, but you have a deal."

I thought to myself, *I was only going to kill you if you wasted anymore of my time.* When the contracts were all signed and money and keys had traded hands he extended his hand to me one last time, we shook hands and parted company.

I walked up to Mark and said, "You drive the Ford back to the motel and I will follow you."

On the way back to the motel I began to run the scenarios through my head as to why Jim was in the shooter's apartment. I kept coming to the same conclusion; he was working with the agency to have me eliminated. I was so angry by the time we got back to the motel I could no longer think straight. When I walked up to the truck Mark was driving he had already began to pull my bags out of the truck. He said, "Let's get your stuff up to the room and sort through your other stuff and leave it in the room."

We entered our room and sorted through the suitcase and found an additional transmitter in the lining of the suitcase. I wasn't sure why I was being tracked or even who it was that was tracking me but I knew someone had marked me. In my profession a marked man doesn't last long.

I lay in bed looking up at the ceiling in the room and continued trying to decide why Jim would be working with the agency. Somewhere during my thought process my eyes got heavy and I woke up to a shake of the shoulder the next morning. Mark was standing over me and said, "The other two are already up and have headed down to the restaurant for breakfast. Do you want to join them?"

I replied, "Sure, let's pack up and when we get to the truck we will transfer the stuff we need to the GMC. Make sure you get the monitor so we can track the other agents and while you are at it slap a couple of transmitters on the ford. Place one under the seat and another under the chassis somewhere."

Mark smiled and said, "I am ahead of you on that, I went down this morning and transferred your case and mine to the GMC, I also transferred the monitor and paperwork. Oh yea, I placed the transmitters under the hood and on the chassis; I will get one more out and put it under the seat. I also turned on the monitor and scanned the position of the other teams; they appear to be stationary at a motel out on the other end of town."

I smiled as Mark seemed to be back on top of his game and I replied, "Mark, I am glad you are with us."

Mark corrected me, "I am with you, the other two are on their own until I know whether we can trust them or not."

We carried our stuff to the truck and headed for the restaurant. Inside the restaurant Mack and Jim were seated in the corner, as we approached Jim saw us, grinned and said, "You old timers finally get the stiffness worked out enough to come down the stairs?"

I chuckled and replied, "We used the elevator, or walkers were too wide for the stairwell."

With that being said we joined Mack and Jim for breakfast. After we ordered Mack asked, "What is the game plan for today?"

I replied, "We are going to split up and travel in two separate vehicles."

Jim looked up from his breakfast and said, "Why separate vehicles?"

Mark replied, "In case we have to split up and follow both of the SUVs, we will be able to tale both vehicles and monitor their activity better."

Mark must have stayed up half the night preparing his answer. It was so good that neither Jim nor Mack questioned it. Our food arrived and Mark and I wolfed our food down so as to not cause a delay. When we were all finished eating and the check had been paid, we headed out to the parking lot. Mack asked, "What are we going to do now?"

I responded, "You guys get your stuff together and let's get rolling."

Mark got in on the driver's side of the GMC and said, "Chris, I need a set of keys for this bucket of bolts if I am going to be chauffeuring you around."

Reaching into my pocket I flipped the keys toward the truck. Mark pulled the keys for the Ford and tossed them in my direction and said, "The boys will need these."

As Mack appeared in the parking lot I called him over and said, "Here are the keys to the Ford, make sure you guys stay up with us and flash your lights if you need to talk."

Mack replied, "How are we going to stay in contact if we have to follow the other SUV?"

I handed Mack one of the cell phones I had just purchased and said, "Only call if it is an emergency, I have preloaded my new number into your phone and be careful."

Mack took the phone and replied, "Sure dad thanks a lot."

I couldn't tell him about Jim until I was able to determine why he was in the picture in the shooter's room. I had been trying to determine if maybe the paper had assigned him to an undercover story, but that wouldn't make sense. He would have told me if that was the case or at least Mr. Clarkston would have let me know. I wasn't sure whom I could trust anymore. In the agency if you lose trust of your partner you are reassigned a new partner. A reassignment now was out of the question. Besides if the agency has to reassign more than one partner you are tagged as paranoid and nobody wants to work with you. Was I being paranoid? I don't think so; I know what I saw in the pictures. Mark called out to me and said, "Let's hit the road."

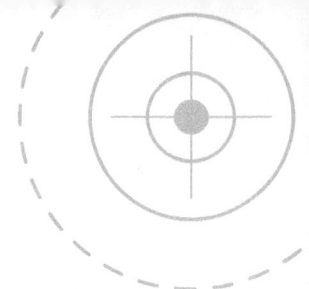

CHAPTER 21

TURNING THE TABLE

We had only been on the road for a short time when Mark suggested we turn on the monitor. I was so wrapped up trying to determine what was going on and trying to put two and two together that I hadn't even given the remaining agents any thought. I reached for the monitor and turned it on. Now there were extra bleeps on the screen, with the additional transmitters we placed in the other pick up. I looked to Mark and said, "I never realized that the transmitters couldn't be filtered out. We will have to remember not to allow Jim or Mack to view this monitor."

Mark replied, "I am sure we can keep them from viewing the monitor, but what about the other agents?"

"I'm sorry Mark; my mind isn't on our mission."

Mark tapped the brakes and said, "Do I need to pull over somewhere and let you get a game plan going?"

"I don't see a need for that; my only concern is that we are eliminating these teams without provocation."

Mark demanded, "Wait just one minute, you will have to explain that last statement if you expect any additional assistance from me."

"The agent that was attempting to escape at the roadblock which Mack eliminated was alive when I reached him. He said that the agency was taking me into protective custody until the agents in Texas were killed, then the order to eliminate me was put into place."

Mark looked discussed with me and said, "Since when have you started listening to propaganda?"

I replied, "He was on his deathbed, what would he gain by lying to me?"

Mark answered, "If he got you eliminated, he completed his mission. Besides it appears you have forgot how you found me. The agents at my house were not attempting to take me into protective custody, were they?"

Realizing that a dying man took me in I replied, "I'm sorry Mark, I told you I wasn't thinking straight. Wondering if killing out our old crew was the right thing to do had added a lot of pressure on my shoulders. A concern about Jim's connection to the agents has pushed me over the top. I wish I knew why he was in the shooter's room."

Mark said, "Why don't we ask him?"

I replied, "There is more to this than just asking Jim about his involvement, we still need some additional questions answered. For example who bugged my equipment and who can I trust."

Mark's concern showed in his eyes when he looked over in my direction and he said, "You can count on me. Between the two of us we will be able to keep you alive."

Mark's assurance was what I was looking for and I replied, "Let's get this thing over."

Mark smiled and said; "Now you are talking!"

I turned my focus back to concentrating on the immediate problem at hand. I watched the bleeps on the screen; they were on the move again. We were only a few miles behind them. As we got closer to the SUVs, close enough for a visual we noticed city police were accompanying them, what a bizarre twist of events. The police were fighting them less than one state away and now they are protecting them. Mark said,

"Why are the police surrounding them? It is almost as though they are giving them an escort."

I replied, "Perhaps they have found a way to convince the police that they are still actively working for the government. If that is the case, I wonder how long they intend to pursue this hoax."

Mark replied, "We can't afford any action towards them with the police protecting them, we don't want to hurt civilians."

Unconcerned with the agents at the moment my focus turned back to Jim. Something had to be done about Jim, it wasn't fair for Mack to be exposed to danger if Jim gets pressured he may have to eliminate Mack to keep from blowing his own cover. Amid my thoughts Mark said, "Thinking about Jim again?"

"Yes, I was thinking about Jim. Well, actually I was thinking more about Mack being left with Jim, if something comes up where Jim's cover is in jeopardy he might have to take Mack out."

Mark said, "That hangs it, if we can't trust our team any longer we will have to confront him or eliminate him."

Knowing Mark was right, as always, I replied, "O.K. let's ask him why he was in the apartment, if the story doesn't check out we will have to eliminate him from the team."

Mark suggested, "Let's pull over at a roadside park where we could discuss this with minimal distractions."

I agreed we headed down the highway until we came to the first roadside park; we pulled over, got out and walked over to a picnic table. Mark walked past the table and leaned against a tree. Mack and Jim joined us as soon as they realized what we were doing. I had taken the pictures, which Mark had enhanced and carried them with me. As soon as Mack was in range to be heard he asked, "So what is up with the police and the other agents?"

I replied, "I think they were able to convince the local authorities that they were working for the government."

Mack said, "Then the local authorities don't talk much with the State patrol."

"Perhaps the local authorities chose to give them the benefit of the doubt. What do you think Jim?"

Jim replied, "I really don't have any thoughts on this subject."

Mark was poised to pull his weapon if needed and was using his cigarette as a cover to provide him with distance from the group. I looked into Jim's eyes and asked, "Why didn't you tell us you were in the shooters apartment?"

Jim's face paled for a minute then he replied, "Can we talk about this in private?"

I answered, "No Jim, I really need an honest and direct answer and I need it now."

Jim replied, "I was working undercover for the paper, we were in the process of infiltrating your old organization when Warren put a hit out on you." I was working with the New York operatives when the orders were received. Robert Jennings and I went to the shooters apartment as soon as we found out you were targeted. Jennings said he had done some things in the past that he wasn't proud of, but he would never assassinate one of his own. He and I went immediately to the building across from yours and began a floor-to-floor search. We found the shooter's room and went in and rendered him unconscious. We carried him out of the room and turned him over to an FBI agent friend of Mr. Clarkston. That is how we found out about the agents that had already been taken out and also which agents were targeted. When we turned him over we immediately went to your room to make sure you were all right. When we came back down stars we saw the police escorting you out of the building."

I asked, "I am suppose to believe what you are saying is the truth?"

Jim explained, "I would hope you would believe me. We followed you to the police station and waited on you to come out of headquarters. We followed you back to the photo shop where you picked up your prints and tried to make contact with you, but you got into a taxi before we could catch up to you. From there we followed you to the New York Times building, at that point I suggested to Jennings that I could handle the surveillance and he should go home and get some rest. The rest of the story is history, I have been with you every since."

Mark couldn't hold back any longer, he flipped his cigarette butt into the air and said, "You expect Chris to believe that pile of rubbish? If you were so intent on helping Chris why didn't you tell him from the beginning that you had rescued him from the shooter and that you had infiltrated our organization?"

Before Jim could answer Mark's questions I interrupted, "Easy Mark, I believe him."

Mark swung around to me his mouth agape and he said, "You have got to be kidding me!"

I replied, "No, Mark, it makes sense now. I remember when I got into the cab to go to the newspaper that the cabby stated a couple of guys seemed as though they were trying to catch me. When I glanced back I remember now that one of those men was Jim."

Mark said, "That doesn't mean that what he is saying is true, only that he has made up an excuse for you seeing him when you got into the taxi. What about the bugs in your pistol handle and luggage and holster, did Jim give you all that stuff?"

Jim threw his hands up in the air and said, "Okay, Okay you caught me, I am a spy and all I ever wanted was to kill Chris that is why I saved his life in the alley at your house. About the bugs in the pistol and other things, I know nothing about that; the FBI gave the material to Mack and me. Mack can collaborate this part of the story."

All eyes turned to Mack and he responded, "That's right, I was there when they handed us the material, they said it would save us time without shopping for the things you were going to need. In addition, they provided us with the 9mm pistols and harnesses."

"SHOOT!" I exclaimed.

I heard the chamber fill in Mark's pistol and he said, "Who?"

Spinning around Mark was already in the prone position and was waiting for a target. I said, "Wait a minute Mark, I didn't mean shoot, what I meant was that we were up against the FBI in this thing. That explains why they were in Nebraska when we called the police in to help. We need to get the bugs out of the weapons and harnesses and we also need to get the bugs off the Ford."

Mack said, "What bugs, what are you talking about?"

I reached out my hand in his direction and said, "Let me see your weapon."

Mack complied and handed me his pistol. I quickly removed the handle from the pistol and produced the first bug. As I was preparing to toss it into the trash, Mack positioned for me to hand the device to him. After a rather lengthy examination he stated, "This device is a positioning device not a listening device."

We began to go through the equipment that Jim and Mack had received from the FBI and we removed seven devices. While we were busy removing and evaluating the devices Mark was clearing the Ford of the bugs we placed. As this exercise was almost complete Jim said, "Chris, I am concerned that you would wait so long before confronting me with any suspensions you had of me. I have tried to prove my worth every since I began helping you."

Rather than be taken in with Jim's hurt feelings I replied, "You weren't altogether honest with us. You knew that you were in the shooter's room and that I was the initial target. Rather than let me know from the beginning you ran some form of masquerade and only informed me of half-truths. So don't get your feelings hurt because Mark and I had concerns about trusting you, just thank your lucky stars that we didn't choose to eliminate you without giving you an opportunity to defend yourself."

Jim didn't like hearing the cold hard truth. I continued, "I guess you thought because you saved my life and felt as though you were fighting for me that I should trust you explicitly. That type of trust is not awarded on how many times you save someone's life rather how much time you spend with each other placing your life in their hands without fear of failure or betrayal. Mark understands that type of trust and so do I, but if anyone should have their feelings hurt or feel betrayed it is Mark and I."

I could tell Jim didn't take this scolding well, but at least he was still alive and could learn from his mistakes. That is more opportunity than Mark would have afforded him.

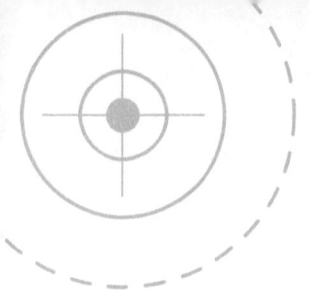

CHAPTER 22

CAT AND MOUSE

With the matter of Jim's fate being put aside we still had a mission to complete. I decided the first thing we should do was to get rid of the Ford pickup and join back up as one team. Now that we could no longer be monitored by outside eyes we could focus on the task that was still before us. I was to the point now that I thought maybe we should just drive up beside the other agents' vehicles and do a drive by like shooting. I no longer had any desire to complete the mission. I was certain if I felt like this the others probably did as well.

We pulled out of the roadside park and headed away from Salina. We pulled into the farming town of Miltonville and abandon the truck in front of the local mortician's office. It seemed at the time to be a good place to leave an old friend. After getting Mack's and Jim's gear from the truck and wiping it down we all migrated back into the GMC. As we turned around on the cobble-stoned main street I marveled at a town that appeared to be untouched since the early nineteen thirties.

Driving back into Salina there was no conversation until Mack said what we were all thinking, "Are we going to complete this mission or what?"

It was important to complete the mission just to eliminate the threat that our past would come back to haunt us if we didn't. Jim said, "Not completing this mission is not an option for any of us. If we don't finish what we started they will finish us."

I replied, "There is your answer Mack, Jim has spoke the gospel on this one. If we don't finish what we started we will be looking over our shoulders the rest of your lives."

Mark interrupted, "And that will be different how?"

Mark's sarcasm is sometimes quite insightful. He truly understands the business we both chose and still has the ability to think rationally so I decided it was time to turn the final operation over to him. I said, "Mark is right. Mark is always right. So Mark I think you should plan the final assault on these teams since you can still reason without being emotionally involved."

Mark said, "Then stop the truck, we need to back track."

I insisted, "What are you talking about?"

Mark replied, "Do you want me to plan this thing or don't you?"

"I want you to plan this thing, but it would be nice to know what it is you are planning."

Mark smiled and said, "We are going back after the Ford, Mack and Jim will take the Ford follow us back to the road-side park pick up the bugs and head to Maryland, just outside D.C. and wait on us. You and I will monitor the other agents' vehicles and track them as they follow Mack and Jim."

I asked, "How will we know where Mack and Jim are at all times?"

Mark said, "Besides calling them on the phones, we can monitor them with this."

Mark pulled a tracking device out of his pocket, activated it and slapped it on the seat between us.

Jim asked, "So you are going to use us for a decoy."

Mark responded, "I wouldn't call you a decoy, rather the lead team. You will draw the agents out of the protection of the Kansas police and assist us into delivering them into the afterlife."

MANHATTAN SHOOTING

Mack replied, "We could set up anywhere along the way and wait on them to drive into our trap and snipe them off before they knew what hit them."

Mark answered, "First we need to ensure they will follow you. The only way to guarantee that they will follow you is to make them think that we are going after their contact in Washington."

Jim said, "I am not sure if we should split up. It is still our job to protect Chris."

Mark said, "Chris will be in good hands, I would be more worried about how much involvement the FBI has in this effort and whether or not they are going to intervene."

As we drove back towards Miltonville the fact that we had some sort of a plan was calming to me and I found myself dozing off. We were sitting in front of the morgue when I awoke. Mack shook my arm and said, "We are about to head towards Washington, I just wanted to shake your hand and wish you luck."

I looked up at Mack's face the sincerity was overwhelming. I laughed for a moment and said, "Mack don't worry, we will be seeing each other sooner than you think."

On our way back to the road-side park Mark suggested we turn on the monitor and take a look and see if the transmitter we placed in the Ford was working. I reached into the back seat and pulled the case that held the monitor into the front seat and opened it and turned it on. It was a good thing that I did. Not only was the transmitter for the Ford working but so were the two transmitters we placed in the agents' vehicles and they were less than eight miles away from us. I instantly picked up the phone and called Jim. When Jim answered I said, "Stop the truck, turn around and get going towards Maryland, the operation is in full swing and the sting is defiantly working."

I could hear through the phone Jim telling Mack to turn around then Jim asked, "How much time do we have?"

I replied, "You have all the time in the world, they are about six miles from us and closing fast. I will let you know when you are at least thirty minutes ahead of them."

Mack and Mark had both turned around, as Mack went speeding back through Miltonville, Mark and I chose this moment to move in behind the agents vehicles. We knew they didn't have a bug in our truck and we could easily monitor Mack and Jim's progress. Mark pulled off on one of the three streets in town and turned around in front of the coop and we sat and waited on the agents to pass. We were only sitting for a short time when the bleeps on the monitor passed our location. I turned on the grid measure and looked over at Mark and said, "Let's give them a three mile head start and then begin to follow them."

Mark asked, "Are Jim and Mack in the clear?"

I replied, "They are about ten miles in front of these clowns, don't worry about Mack, one thing he can do well is drive."

Mark backed the truck up to leave the parking lot and we began to follow the bleeps on the screen. I turned the volume down on the monitor so that the constant pinging would not drive Mark stark raving mad. As we entered Nebraska I knew this was going to turn into a cat and mouse game. I looked over at Mark and asked, "Do you have a plan B?"

Mark smiled and replied; "I haven't seen anything wrong with plan A at this point."

We had only been on the road for about three hours and by that time Mack and Jim had increased their lead by over twenty miles. I was preparing to make this comment to Mark when the phone rang, I answered and it was Jim. He said, "We are about out of gas and really need to pull over and fill up, how much time do we have?"

I looked at the grids and calculated the distance and replied, "You have about a twenty two mile lead. Are you near a town now?"

Jim replied, "I don't know about being near a town but we are pulling into a truck stop."

I answered, "Hurry, I will call you back if they close within ten miles of you."

Mark said, "We might as well stop and get gas too, it may be the last chance we have for a while."

Mark began to speed up, when I cautioned, "Unless your plan is to pass the agents ahead of us you better take your foot out of it."

Mark slowed back down and we quickly began to lag the agents by three to five miles. Mack and Jim were back on the road with about a fifteen-mile lead. I began to relax a bit.

We had been driving for about fifteen minutes when the bleeps from the agents' vehicles came to a stop. I said, "Looks as though they needed some gas too."

Mark slowed again and asked, "Do you want me to stop and wait here until they get back on the road?"

I replied, "No, they aren't aware of the vehicle we are driving and there is no way for them to be monitoring us. Let's pull into the truck stop and fuel up ourselves and maybe pick up some snacks for the road."

Mark nodded his acknowledgement and sped back up.

As we pulled into the truck stop the agents were already returning to their vehicles, it looked as though their agenda didn't include anything other than overtaking Mack and Jim. We pulled up to the gas pumps and Mark began to fuel the truck. I watched as the agents headed their vehicles back to the highway. When they had cleared my view I relaxed and looked over to Mark and asked, "Do you think Mack and Jim are good enough to hold them off until we arrive?"

Mark replied, "They are both grown men and both knew what they were getting themselves in for when they accepted this assignment."

I answered, "I know they are grown men, but it was because of me that they are even involved in this mess."

Mack completed refueling the truck and he and I went inside the truck stop. We went up and down the snack isles gathering food for the trip. Mack stopped by the soft drink cooler and pulled a twelve pack of soda, we had wasted about eight minutes in the truck stop which placed us about ten miles behind the agents. We paid the cashier and headed back to the truck. Nearing the truck, I could hear the cellular phone ringing. We had left it in the truck. I rushed over to answer; Mack was on the line, he asked, "Are we far enough ahead of the agents to risk the line at the toll both?"

I grabbed the monitor and flipped it on; Mack and Jim were still about fifteen miles in front of the agents. I replied, "You have about a fifteen mile head start, you be the judge."

I slid across to the passenger seat and Mark and I were on our way. Mark knew that if we allowed the agents to overtake Mack and Jim that our chances for successfully completing the mission would be greatly reduced. Even though Mark or I either one would admit openly that we were too old for this business we both knew we were. About five minutes had passed before Mack and Jim began to move again, I hoped that their lead could be increased when the other agents approached the turnpike.

Mark and I were about eighteen miles behind the agents and the agents were still closing in on Mack and Jim. I picked up the phone and called Mack. When he answered, I said, "You guys need to pick it up a little, the agents are sitting in your back pocket."

Mack replied, "I know we can see the SUVs behind us when we come to the straight parts of the turnpike."

Concerned with their safety I made the decision to not get on the turnpike put to take the business loop instead. I looked over at Mark and said, "Let's see what this truck can do."

Mark pressed the accelerator solid to the floorboard and we began to increase speed. We were going about one hundred and five miles an hour and had finally started to make up time on the agents. Turning back to the phone I said, "Mack, you and Jim need to take the next available exit onto the business loop, when we get close enough

I will call you back and we will try and get the agents in a crossfire situation."

Mack agreed. I could tell by the stress in his voice that he was tired of this cat and mouse game and was ready for a show down. We watched the monitor as Mack and Jim exited the turnpike. They were still several miles ahead of the agents. After what seemed an eternity the agents exited the turnpike and headed in the Jim and Mack's direction.

We were moments behind the agents by now and their lead decreased slightly as they paid their way off of the turnpike. As Mark accelerated to overtake the agents I asked, "So, do you have a plan yet?"

Mark smiled and said, "When I catch up to them you eliminate them. Simple plan, don't you agree?"

I replied, "I guess it will have to work, we really don't have a lot of options."

Still working out the details of our next step in my mind, Mark replies, "Are you ready?"

I answered, "As ready as I will ever be." Directly in front of our pick up was the trailing SUV, these agents didn't have any idea that they were being followed. They actually thought they had the upper hand and were going to use surprise to their advantage. I almost felt sorry for them. Without thinking anymore about strategy we pulled alongside of the trailing SUV, I rolled down the window and began shooting. The driver was the first to be hit; slumping over the steering wheel the vehicle began to speed up. As the vehicle careened out of control and onto the shoulder of the road I could see the agent adjacent to the driver attempting to take control of the vehicle. I thought he was going to be successful when the front of the vehicle collided with a light pole; we were able to narrowly escape the end of the pole from slamming into my truck.

I dialed Mack and Jim's cellular number and waited for them to answer. Unsure when the lead SUV would realize that the trailing vehicle was disabled. Mack answered the phone. He said, "Are you about ready for us to slow down and let the agents catch up so we can catch them in the crossfire?"

I replied, "We have already confronted one of the vehicles and have eliminated the agents in that vehicle. We are now in a two on one situation."

Mack made a boyish sound of glee and replied, "What do you need us to do?"

I replied, "Find the nearest exit, pull off the highway and get ready to assist with disabling the other SUV."

I could hear Mack relaying the last plan to Jim and then Mack said, "I guess this will be over with soon."

I replied, "The immediate threat will be over but we still have some work to finish in Washington D.C."

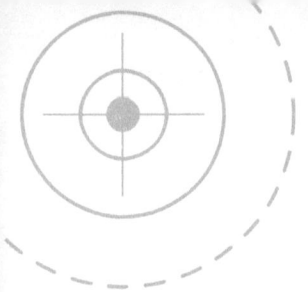

CHAPTER 23

TURNING THE TIDE

Things had suddenly taken an unexpected turn. The highway was lined with squad cars and rather than targeting the rogue agents they were targeting us. The first round ripped through the windshield barely missing Mark's head. Mark said, "It looks like these agents have figured out a way to call in some help."

I replied, "Let's get off the main highway and see how these boys handle their own streets."

Mark did as I asked and we were racing down city streets. I called Mack to let them know that they needed to find a way to intercept us so they could get out of the decoy truck and join us. Mack suggested we attempt to meet near the center of the city. Abandon the vehicles and commandeer a suitable substitute. As Mark swerved in and out of traffic he was beginning to put some distance between the pursuing officers and us. Nearing downtown Mark swung into a parking garage near a large mall. He found the first available parking spot and pulled in. We quickly grabbed our equipment and headed up to the next level of the garage. Mark took the time to wipe the vehicle down; old habits are hard to break.

On the next level of the garage we found a panel van, which had a long distance providers name plastered on the side. Mark quickly manipulated the locks and worked his magic on the ignition. Within minutes we were mobile again. As we were exiting the parking garage the police were arriving. They had already blocked the entrance to the garage and were on their way to secure the exits. Mark commented, "Good thing we chose the van."

I couldn't believe how cool Mark remained during this entire episode. I was having a hard time thinking one step ahead, Mark seemed as though he had this entire escape planned in advance. As we got closer to the downtown area I picked up the phone and dialed Mack. Mack said, "We are sitting outside a Starbuck's waiting on you."

I replied, "A street name or an address would be nice."

Mack answered, "We are sitting on the corner on Main and Chesnee."

I looked over to Mark, repeated the address and replied back to Mack, "Mark wants his black; I would appreciate cream and sugar in mine. We will be there in less than ten minutes."

Approaching downtown we turned on Main; we were about two blocks from Chesnee, Mark asked, "Did you tell them we were in a phone company truck?"

"No, I figured they would be watching for us and would recognize your ugly mug."

Mark grinned and said, "If they don't, you will have to get out and get them."

Nearing Starbuck's Mack and Jim ran over to the panel van and jumped into the back with their equipment in tow. As Jim settled into the back of the van he handed Mark a cup of coffee and said, "You guys owe me three bucks each."

Mark and I laughed as we took our coffee and I replied, "It's good to see you guys too."

Now that we were the hunted instead of the hunter I suggested we should get to a used car dealership and pick up another vehicle. Mark pulled along the outside of a dealership and let me out, he said, "We will go up a couple of blocks and start wiping down the vehicle and get everything ready to make the swap."

I agreed and headed towards the dealership. Inside the showroom were several salespeople sitting at their desk. I stood waiting on one of the vultures to swoop down on me and try a hard sale. Instead everyone remained lifeless and seemed disinterested in helping me find the vehicle of my dreams. Rather than stand around for several minutes I found my way out onto the car lot. I found a low mileage truck with four doors that would meet our needs and opened the door. The truck was set up with all the bells and whistles. As I was backing out of the truck a young ladies voice rang out, "May I help you?"

I looked around at a fairly attractive young lady and replied, "If you can get this truck transferred into my name in the next fifteen minutes you certainly may help me."

She smiled and said, "If you have the right credit I can make the deal."

I replied, "Unless you try to rob me on this truck I am willing to pay cash."

She asked me to follow her into her office and we could get the paperwork filled out. We had spent about five minutes haggling over the price before we reached an agreement. It took about another eleven minutes for the final signatures to be signed and Tom Smith had just purchased his third vehicle this year. As I was walking out of the office the young lady called after me saying, "I hope you enjoy your truck Mr. Smith."

Glancing back I thanked her and headed out to the car lot. I started the truck and headed out of the parking lot. I dialed the other cellular phone and Mack answered in a low whisper, "The police are at the van, we are one block away heading west."

As I neared the street where the van was abandon the police were at scene trying to find some sort of evidence or clue as to our whereabouts. I continued heading west and speaking into the phone I said, "O.K. I have passed the van, now where are you." Mack said we are two blocks from the van and will be turning north, hurry we won't go undetected long."

Swinging the pickup onto the second street passed the van I noticed the guys loaded down with equipment and suitcases. Nearing their location, they threw their belongings into the truck and we were together and mobile once again. Mark looked at me and said, "Your right, I am getting to old for this type of excitement."

"How did you guys get away without being detected by the police?"

Jim answered, "We had pulled off onto a side street like we had planned. Mark insisted we start wiping the van down so we would be ready to go when you got here. An old lady that lived in the house we parked in front of came out and told us to move the van. Mack told her if she wanted the van moved to call the police and have them move it. I guess she did."

Looking over at Mack I demanded, "Why would you say something so stupid? Didn't you know she would call the police?"

Mack replied, "Of course I knew she would call the police. I figured as long as we knew where the police were going to be that we could buy enough time to get out of town undetected."

"I'm not sure I like your plan, but the end result seemed to have worked out."

Mark added, "If it hadn't worked out I was going to shoot him before the police could.

Have you ever tried to climb a fence holding two suitcases and a briefcase?"

As we headed out of town Jim turned on the monitor. The agents we were following were almost off the screen. They appeared to be heading to D.C. Jim said, "Are we still going to try and take them out?"

I replied, "No, I think it is time we planned on taking out the source. There are one or two men, which must be eliminated to end this thing, Paul Warren and Larry Brown."

Mark injected, "Larry, what is Larry's involvement in this thing?"

I answered, "Larry is the one that leaked that lousy cover story on the first two agents we eliminated. Unless he was trying to help our old agency cover things up, why would he leak a cover story for their death?"

Mark replied, "Perhaps to assist you from being detected."

"I don't think so; Larry wouldn't have any reason to go out on a limb for me."

Jim added, "Isn't it possible that Larry was acting on orders from the President? After all he is the one that we are actually working for on this whole thing."

Mack interrupted the conversation and he said, "Hey, I don't know about the rest of you guys but I could use some food."

Food sounded good to me and it must have sounded good to everybody else because there were no objections to Mack's request. We had passed the border to Maryland and decided to stop at the first restaurant.

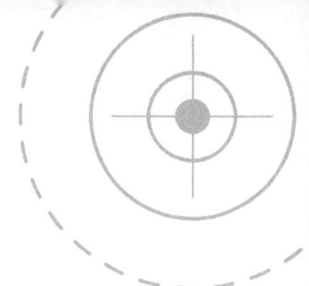

CHAPTER 24

STANDING DOWN

Inside the restaurant I was still feeling uneasy about Larry Brown's involvement in this assignment. While everyone was waiting on their orders to be brought to the table I slipped outside for a smoke and decided to call the President. I was surprised when the phone was answered directly by the President instead of one of his aides. I said, "Mr. President, this is Chris Moore and I need some help on completing the mission you assigned me."

To my amazement the President replied, "Chris I have been expecting your call, there has been much misinformation leaked here in Washington about your mission. The FBI was hunting you until about an hour ago when I pulled them off your trail. Seems someone had accused you and your team of being terrorists. Several law enforcement groups are hunting you even now. I have my aides working with the major law enforcement groups to put a stop to their actions. It may take some time. It is imperative that you do not confront any of the law enforcement organizations, we wouldn't be able to cover up the death of any additional police."

I said, "Additional police? We haven't shot any police."

The President replied, "I never said your team had shot any police, however several police have died because of the renegade agents you are eliminating. I would like for you and your team to stand down for now until we can find who is feeding the disinformation and get the civilian law enforcement to drop their involvement."

I assured the President that we would stand down; he asked that we check with him at least once a week to verify any progress that his aides had made. I felt as though we should stay active since we were so close to closing this entire operation but I was not going to go against the wishes of the Commander and Chief.

Back inside the restaurant the food had already been delivered to the table. A big steak and fries was exactly what I needed. I began to eat my meal when Mack asked where I had been. I replied, "I was talking to the President on the phone. He has asked us to stand down until the civilian law enforcement can be backed off of us and until the President's aides can locate the source of the disinformation which is being fed to the civilian officials."

Mark set his fork on the corner of his plate and said, "Why would we stand down now, we are so close to completing the assignment?"

I answered, "It is no longer our call, the President has asked us to step down, so until he changes his mind I guess we can buy some fishing gear and go camping. I don't want to be trapped in a city that I am not familiar with and not be able to escape."

Jim said, "Fishing sounds great to me, I could use some rest and relaxation, after all Mack and I are still on the payroll."

During the meal we discussed the things we would need for camping in the woods. We decided we would get enough provisions to last us a week and then would play it by ear from there. Mark suggested we go to Conowingo Reservoir; he had an Uncle that owned a cabin there and only used it for a couple of weeks out of the year. When the plans were complete and our meals were finished we got in the truck and headed for Cecil County.

Pulling into Cecil County we found a store that had the supplies we needed. Everyone was counting on catching fish for the meat we needed rather than to stock up on steaks and chicken. I went ahead and put a variety of meats, including lunchmeats into the cart. As everyone was gathering their last items I said, "O.K. we only have one thing to worry about now."

All eyes were on me and I continued, "The game warden, we can't take a chance on buying fishing licenses and being tracked to this area."

A chorus of chuckles came from the group as we paid for your supplies. After everything was loaded into the truck Mack spoke up, "Do you guys want fish for supper?"

Mark replied, "Only if you filet what you catch. I hate eating fish and dodging the bones."

The conversation continued along this path as everyone was stating their preferences of fish preparation. We pulled into Mark's uncle's cabin around three in the afternoon. We had put everything away and decided we would go try out the fishing. Unfamiliar with the type of fish in the lakes in Maryland, I decided to try a plastic worm. After several minutes of fishing I got my first hit. It was a black bass about fifteen inches long. I fished for several hours and got two more keepers. Growing weary of standing along the bank I decided to head to the cabin and clean the fish I had caught.

As I neared the cabin I got an uneasy feeling. I wasn't sure if the feelings I was having was due to guilt I was feeling for not completing my assignment or if perhaps there was danger waiting at the cabin. I decided to trust my instincts rather than blow them off. I found a clearing in the woods that I could remain concealed in and still view the backside of the cabin. I sat and waited, trying to find anything that was out of the normal. I remained concealed for about twenty minutes until I felt a hand plant gently on my shoulder. My heart rose into my throat, I twirled around to come face to face with Mark and his big dumb grin. He said, "You can't let these fish stay out of water much longer, either clean them or put them back in the lake."

The fish, I had forgotten about the fish. I replied, "Mark, you almost caused me to have a heart attack. How did you know I was here?"

Mark replied, "I didn't, I heard your fish flouncing around on the ground and came over to see what the noise was all about. Why are you standing here?"

"As I was headed to the cabin to clean the fish I got an uneasy feeling. I decided to watch the cabin and make sure everything was alright before I went on up."

Mark asked, "Well, did you plan on watching all day until you get the nerve to go check things out?"

"Nerve is not the issue here. The last time I ignored my instincts I stood in front of my apartment window and was nearly eliminated. I have always been able to rely on me. If I am wrong the only one that gets hurt here are these fish."

Mark looked deep into my face and said, "You are really bothered by this aren't you? Do you want me to go check out the house?"

I replied, "I don't think that is necessary. I was about to move up to the cabin anyway, I had just about convinced myself that everything is alright anyway."

Mark knelt down next to the fish and said, "Old friend, seldom do I apologize for anything but I feel as though I owe you an apology."

"What for scarring my sox off of my feet?"

Mark lowered his voice and said, "No, there is someone sneaking through the woods at the other corner of the house."

I turned my focus towards the perimeter of the woods and watched for movement. It wasn't long until I spotted the object. Sure enough someone was slinking through the woods watching the cabin. Mark tapped me on the shoulder and said, "Give me ten minutes to get into position and then walk up towards the cabin. I will take this joker out if he makes any move in your direction."

I agreed and began the wait for ten minutes to pass. When ten minutes had passed I picked up the fish and began moving into the opening. I expected at anytime to hear the sound of Mark's pistol discharge. I reached the back of the cabin and hung my stringer of fish on a nail tacked to the back porch. I hesitated at the door to inspect it and ensure Mack hadn't placed any of his little toys on the door. When I was convinced it was safe I entered the cabin. As I maneuvered my way to a bedroom window I peered out in an attempt to see what became of Mark. I had crouched at the window as to keep myself as small as possible in case someone wanted to use me for target practice. Looking out the window into the woods I could see no movement. The shade on the porch created shadows, which didn't allow me to get a good view of the woods. As I began to position myself to move to another window I heard the back door open. Peering out of the bedroom towards the backdoor I saw Mark with his arm on the shoulder of an elderly gentleman. Mark called out, "Chris, it's alright, it was just my uncle trying to find out who had invaded his cabin."

With a sigh of relief I replied, "I guess that means I should get those fish cleaned."

I introduced myself to Mark's uncle and apologized for dropping in unannounced. Mark's uncle was gracious, he said, "Don't worry about it, any friend of my nephew is a friend of mine."

Slipping out onto the back porch I began to filet the fish I had caught. As I was completing the job on the first fish Mark's Uncle Bill showed up holding a tray. He said, "Just slap the filets on this tray, I already have the grease in the cooker getting warm. That is of course if I am invited to share a meal with you boys."

I replied, "If you are willing to cook them I am more than willing to share. Hopefully these aren't the only fish which will be caught today, Mack and Jim are still down by the lake."

Bill pulled a chair away from the back of the cabin wall and sat down. After he propped his feet on the porch rail he said, "Are you boys in trouble?"

Not knowing what Mark had shared with his uncle I replied, "Why would you think we were in trouble?"

Bill continued, "Well, every time I get a visit from Mark it is because he is trying to rest up from one of his missions or he just needs a place to come and think before continuing with whatever mission he is on. Of course I haven't seen him since the agency pushed him into early retirement."

Mark was standing at the door listening to his uncle, he came onto the porch and said, "Uncle Bill I thought we had an understanding, if I tell you something you keep it to yourself."

Bill grinned and said, "It's alright boy, I can tell this guy is an agent." I interrupted, "What makes you think I am an agent?"

Bill said, "I never said I think you are an agent, I said I can tell you are an agent. I spent thirty years pulling guys like you out of jams when I was working for the CIA."

Mark replied, "Chris don't worry about Uncle Bill he is the reason I got into the business, as a matter of fact if I hadn't spent the summers of my childhood up here at the cabin I wouldn't have even thought about becoming an agent. Besides Uncle Bill still has contacts at the headquarters and still has a lot of clout if we need any information."

I asked, "So Bill, do you know anything about John Clarkston."

Bill replied, "Of course I know Johnny, he was one of the best agents the agency ever had. He really fell into it when he got assigned his last cover as the head of that New York newspaper."

I contested, "You must be crazy, and John Clarkston is not an agent."

Bill said, "O.K. he is not an agent. He is just the luckiest editor in the business that is how he breaks so many news stories when the other papers don't even know anything is a miss. How do you think the agency stays up with the news from inside the states? That's right he tells them through his newspaper, he has been printing all the information the agency needed for years."

Flabbergasted by this startling news I looked to Mark for confirmation. Mark shrugged his shoulders and said, "I can't tell you Chris, I never asked about Clarkston before."

Bill smiled and injected, "It's a little hard to swallow finding out the truth isn't it. Don't worry; he is not the only agent that has the important job of getting information to our agents. There are two network anchors who have been in the agency every since they graduated college, several politicians, a few ex-athletes and a host of judges and lawyers."

I was completing the filet on the last fish when I heard voices coming out of the woods, Bill asked, "Are they with you?"

Glancing in the direction of the voices I noticed Jim and Mack coming across the opening, I replied, "Yes they are with me."

Bill said, "Good, if those trout boxes have any fish in them, I won't be forced to eat these bass."

When Mack and Jim got close enough to speak without shouting the bragging began. I sat the filet knife on the porch rail and said, "You caught them you clean them!"

Mack said, "Don't you even want to see how many we caught?" I replied, "Not really, I caught all I needed for supper."

Jim and Mack opened their trout boxes and began to pull one fish after another out of their boxes. I guess because they didn't have a fishing license it didn't matter if the fish were too small to keep. When they had finished pulling the trout out to show them off there were several trout with some size, all total there were eleven fish. I started into the cabin when Jim asked, "Who is the old gent on the porch?"

Bill barked, "Old gent, who are you calling old you young punk?"

Jim replied, "I didn't mean any disrespect old timer, I was just curious who you were."

Clearly annoyed by Jim's insistence to refer to Bill as old, Bill set the tray on the porch rail and said, "This old man will roll your head all the way to the woods if you're not careful."

Amused with the spryness Bill was showing, Jim quickly attempted to defuse the situation. He said, "I'm sorry, I didn't mean any disrespect, I was just teasing."

Bill quickly settled down and said, "O.K. you young pup, I won't pin your ears back since you are clearly backing down."

Jim looked at me and asked, "Who is he?"

I opened the back door and replied, "Your host."

I left Jim to deal with Bill and pulled the back door shut. In the kitchen Mark had began peeling potatoes and asked, "Do you know how to make cold slaw?"

I replied, "I can finishing peeling and cutting up those potatoes, but that is about the extent of my kitchen skills."

Mark handed me the knife and went towards the refrigerator and pulled ahead of cabbage out and began chopping. We had finished the cold slaw and began frying the French fries by the time Bill entered the cabin with the fish. He placed the platter on the counter and quickly began moving around the kitchen gathering the ingredients he needed for his fish batter. Before we could ask if he needed any help Bill said, "Out, this kitchen is only big enough for one cook and that is me. So go in the other room and find something to occupy your time."

Without a word of argument I left the kitchen with Mark not far behind. When Jim and Mack had washed up I heard Bill kicking them out of the kitchen as well. Jim came into the living room and said, "I like your uncle, and he is really spry for a man his age."

Bill yelled in from the kitchen and said, "YOU YOUNG PUP, DON'T START IT UP AGAIN."

Jim whispered, "His hearing is keen too."

We had only been sitting in the living room for a short time when Bill announced that supper was ready. As we went into the table in kitchen, Bill had prepared a feast, there were fries, cold slaw, pinto beans, hush puppies, corn on the cob, and fried fish. It was by far the best meal any of us had eaten in over a month. I was so full when I finished eating that after helping clean up the mess in the kitchen I went straight to the bedroom and went to bed. I also had an ulterior motive; there were only two bed rooms, the one I was in with twin beds and the one I was sure Bill was going to use. Minutes after I had crawled into bed I could hear the others trying to decide where they were going to sleep for the night. I closed my eyes and fell asleep.

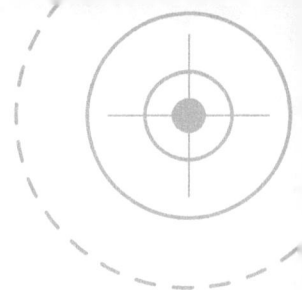

CHAPTER 25

UNINVITED GUEST

The following morning I awoke early and slipped down stairs and out the back door before anyone else was stirring. I grabbed by fishing pole and headed down to the lake. The early morning dew was heavy on the weeds and the water dripped from my legs down inside my shoes and soaked my feet. This turned out to be a good thing because now I wasn't concerned about getting my shoes wet if I felt like wading into the edge of the lake. The water on the lake was like glass. By wading out into the lake a short distance I was able to cast up and down the banks without worrying about catching the branches of the nearby trees. Almost right away the fish began to bite. I had filled my stringer with fish before the sun was up above the trees on the opposite shore.

I started back towards the cabin; again the feeling that something was wrong came over me. I stood at the edge of the woods and surveyed the area before stepping out into the opening between the woods and the cabin. I must be getting paranoid in my old age. I stood for several minutes watching for movement.

Several minutes had passed when I caught movement in the edge of the woods off to my right. I concentrated on the area to try and see what the movement was. Several minutes later in the same area I was watching a deer stepped out into the open field. It held tight against the tree line and nibbled at the tender grass the field had to offer. Growing tired of watching the deer I shift my focus to the other side of the field. I knew the deer wouldn't step out into the open if it felt threatened in any way or if it smelled man. After several more minutes of staring into the dark undercover I decided I was indeed paranoid and really needed to use this time off to relax.

Stepping out into the clearing, the deer to my right was startled and sprang back into the woods. I walked up to the cabin and as I neared, the back door swung open and there was Mark holding me a cup of coffee. The smell of bacon escaped the confines of the cabin and tempted my nostrils. As I drew a deep breath to take in the smell of the morning breakfast Bill called out, "If you are going to eat any of this breakfast you better get washed up."

I hung my stringer on the nail on the back porch and headed into the cabin. I walked passed Jim and Mack without a word and washed my hands. When I came back into the room Bill had already filled my plate and was waiting for me at the edge of the kitchen. As he handed me the plate he reached out patted me on the back and said, "Nice stringer, I will take you out this afternoon and show you where the big fish are hiding."

I took the plate and replied, "I would enjoy that Bill, and thank you for the breakfast."

Bill replied, "Don't mention it, it is my pleasure, I don't get many visitors and the ones I generally get I don't want staying around for long."

I sat at the dining table and began to eat my meal. The feeling that something was not right was still nagging me. I looked over to Mark and said, "Mark, I have that little feeling again."

Mark smiled and said, "Don't worry about it Chris, it is just indigestion."

After breakfast I went out on the back porch to clean my fish but Bill had beat me to the punch. He was finishing the last fish. I said, "Bill, I didn't expect you to clean my fish."

Bill replied, "Chris at this stage in life it is a pleasure to do these little favors, besides I didn't want you to have any excuse for not going fishing with me when I get ready to go."

I exclaimed, "I am willing to go fishing anytime, except right now I have an uneasy feeling."

Bill spoke up, "You have it too? Let's wash the filets and bag them and we will go check the place out."

Inside the cabin Bill began barking orders to Jim and Mack, he said, "You youngsters clean the kitchen and put stuff away, this ain't no resort hotel where the maids take care of your messes."

Bill turned his attention in the direction of Mark and said, "Nephew, wipe your chin and come go with us."

Without any additional orders to bark, Bill turned into the hallway and began walking. I thought he was going after a cap or something so I stood in the dining room and waited. After several more steps down the hallway he turned and said, "Are you coming?"

"Sure," I replied.

Unaware that there were any other exits from the cabin besides the front and back door I followed. Bill paused at the door of a hallway closet for a second, opened the door, entered the closet and remained inside. I delayed approaching for about fifteen seconds, thinking any minute now he would be coming out of the closet with a cap, a rifle, a pair of binoculars or something. When he didn't come back out of the closet I walked towards the open door. As I neared the door Mark grabbed me by the arm and whispered, "Don't freak out, he is a bit exocentric."

Exocentric didn't even come close to describing what was behind that door. A false wall in the side of the closet was open and stairs led down from there. I got to the header of the stairs and Bill yelled up, "Don't forget to close the door."

I did as I was told. The stairs led down into a mini-fortress, this place must have cost Bill thousands of dollars to complete. It was constructed like a military barracks, complete with cots and weapons of all descriptions. I was speechless. Bill looked at me with my mouth agape and said, "That is the same look I got from my wife when the tornado back in eighty-three came through the area and I had her come down for safety."

I asked, "Why would you build such a room under your cabin?"

Bill said, "I have one just like it at my home. When you have been in the game as long as I have you amass quite a few enemies, I don't plan on being eliminated without putting up a good fight."

"How do you plan on defending this area, you chose the low ground, they can sit at the top of the stairs and snipe you from anywhere in this room?"

Bill smiled and walked to the back corner of the room and pulled a lever to open up a passageway. Just inside the passageway was a military plunger. He pointed in the direction of the plunger and said, "They will have a hard time surviving the cabin exploding in on them."

Bill continued through the passageway, the passage was quite long and seemed to go on forever. As the light in the passage began to dim I said, "Does this come out in the middle of the lake?"

Bill laughed and said, "We are almost there."

At the end of the passageway we approached another set of stairs, these were a little more crudely constructed than the ones that led into the mini-fortress but were just as functional. At the top of the stairs was a trap door, which opened into the center of the woods. Bill pulled a key from his pocket and unlocked the door. As soon as we were out of the door he turned back and re-locked the door. The door was made of half-inch steel and was bolted and welded on top of a concrete well shaft. Bill said, "One day while I was coming back to the cabin I found this old water well. I thought at the time it would be a great escape tunnel. After several months of planning and two years of building I completed it. The passageway was all dug by hand."

Amazed at the effort that Bill put into this project, but concerned about the reasoning I said, "Bill you are more paranoid than I am."

Bill looked at me and said very matter-of-factly, "It wasn't luck that allowed an agent of my age to live as long as I have. If you want to call that paranoid then I have been this way all my life and it seems to be working for me."

Mark was growing tired of this show and tell and said, "Now that we are through site seeing can we go back to the cabin?"

Bill said, "Not just yet. Come on to my observation tree, Chris and I feel as though someone is watching us."

We followed Bill further into the woods, at the base of one of the trees was boards hammered into the tree, much like a kid would use for a tree house. At the top of these boards was a tree house. Inside the tree house were a chair and a pair of binoculars. Mark and I sat on the floor and left the chair for Bill. Bill sat down in the chair and pulled the binoculars from the nail in the wall and began to scan towards the cabin. We set silent for several minutes when Bill said, "There is a black SUV sitting up by the lake road. It is not in the parking lot for the ramp and there are no campsites where it is parked."

Mark pulled the binoculars from his uncle's hand and peered towards the SUV. After several minutes he concurred with Bill's observation. "It does look like a government issue."

Mark handed the binoculars to me and pointed in the direction of the SUV. I looked through the glasses and could make out only the top of the SUV. Mark said, "Are you game to walk up there and check things out?"

I replied, "I am willing to walk up there, but how will we know where the agents are if it does turn out to be a government vehicle."

Bill said, "You boys, I don't see how you survived as long as you have without having a clue. I have eyes and ears planted all around the cabin. Just be patient a minute or two and I will locate the invaders."

I sat there for several minutes waiting on Bill to pull out some sort of monitor and listening device, instead he just sat in his chair staring out the window. Finally, I said, "Aren't you going to tell us where your monitor is situated so we can help?"

Bill began to laugh aloud and finally he said, "Chris, the listening and monitor devices are out the window. The deer, the blue jays and magpies, the rabbits and all the other inhabitants of the woods will tell if there are any intruders."

Just as Bill had said, after I began to focus on the woods around the cabin I noticed a rabbit race into the clearing near the back of Bill's cabin. I looked back into the woods from where the rabbit was startled and could see movement. There was someone working his way through the edge of the woods behind the cabin. I pointed in the direction of the movement and said, "There is one of them."

Bill handed me the binoculars and I zoomed in on the intruder's location. I couldn't tell if he was an agent or not, he didn't appear as though he was caring a rifle or anything in his hands. I said, "Well, I guess there must be some sort of leak in our security if they have already tracked us down. There are only five people that know we are here and there are no tracking devices which could have led them to us."

Bill replied, "You are awful conceded if you think you are the only ones the agency sends men to eliminate."

I asked, "What do you mean by that? I don't think they are particularly after just me, I know they are here for Mark and the others."

Bill said, "Maybe, but you are still awful conceded. This wouldn't be the first time that the agency has sent individuals or even teams out here to eliminate me."

Mark asked, "Why would the agency be concerned about you, Uncle Bill?"

Bill replied, "Seems that when the agency thinks you have out lived your usefulness and you don't move into public office then you need to be taken off the payroll permanently. This would not be the first time that agents were sent here to try their level best to have my time clock punched. Last year they sent two men up here, they make a great habitat for the bass. Seems the SUV was just the right size to add enough cover for the fish to hide in."

Mark exclaimed, "You never told me about this!"

Bill continued, "Weren't any need to involve you nephew. Seems the agency wants to test me to make sure I am not getting senile. I am sure that is why they are sending these youngsters after me instead of some seasoned professionals. I dispatch the agents and they leave me alone for a year or at least six months."

I interrupted, "How can you be sure the agents aren't coming for some other reason besides trying to eliminate you?"

Bill said, "About four years ago after I retired from my job in Washington D.C., the first agent showed up. I could tell he was young and I could also tell he was nervous. I invited him into the house and asked him if I could help him with something. It seemed as though he was afraid to complete his mission. Before the conversation could really get going good I realized why he was there, not from anything he had said but from the scared deer in the headlights look that was on his face. I slipped into the kitchen picked up my 9mm and waited on the young man to get the nerve to pull his pistol. We talked for an additional five minutes before I just came right out and asked him why he had been assigned to kill me. I think he was going to answer my question, but I didn't give him the opportunity. When I realized that I was right I eliminated him. I went outside and surveyed the area for his vehicle. When I located it I dug through the vehicle until I found the paperwork authorizing the hit. The authorization was given by Paul Warren."

I exclaimed, "Paul Warren! He is the man we are after. Warren and Larry Brown seem to be the spear head of the whole covert operation."

Bill replied, "I am not surprised, neither of those two ever seemed like the agency type, they were always looking for the easy way out of every assignment I ever gave them. After the first attack I made some

MANHATTAN SHOOTING

inquires into Washington to determine why a hit was put out on me. No one from any of the agencies would admit that I was on any list. Things went back to normal after that for about a year and then one afternoon at my house in Connecticut two agents appeared, these guys were a little more seasoned than the first. They used standard attack procedures. They monitored the house and watched for movement. I began to watch them when my paperboy announced to me that there were two men parked down the street watching my house through binoculars. I played along, when ten o'clock rolled around I turned the lights in the house off and went up stairs to my bedroom, I turned on the light to the bedroom then the bathroom. After several minutes the lights to the bathroom were turned off and finally the bedroom. I worked my way down the hall into the linen closet at the top of the stairs and waited. The agents came in together; I could hear them down stairs setting up their cover. They were opening drawers and moving paperwork so to the police it would seem like a burglary. I appreciated them setting up the cover so that after I shot them I could call the police and the police could dismiss the action as a burglary gone bad. After several minutes they started up the stairs, when I knew they were nearing the bedroom I shot them. One was shot in the back and the other turned just as I fired. I checked them and they were both dead. I wasted no time calling 911 and reporting the break in and shooting. The police dismissed the case as a burglary gone badly and there was not even a grand jury convened. There have been two additional attempts; both times I was able to send the agency the message that I was alive and well."

"It seems as though you somewhat enjoy these visits." Bill answered, "Well it keeps me on my toes."

Mark said, "I don't want to be a kill joy but don't you think someone should find out what this guy is doing here?"

As we were preparing to investigate the individual Jim exited the back of the cabin and began walking towards the woods in the direction of the concealed individual. Mark said, "Looks like Jim has finally shown his true colors."

Unwilling to believe that Jim would betray us I said, "What makes you so sure that he isn't out looking for us or just going down to the lake?"

Mark replied, "He isn't caring a fishing pole and the guy we were watching is walking out of the woods to meet him."

We sat and watched as Jim extended his hand to the stranger and after a few minutes they headed back to towards the cabin together. I said, "We have got to get there before they do or Mack won't stand a chance."

Bill replied, "Here take the key to the tunnel and I will follow along after you to seal everything up behind you."

Mark and I rushed out of the tree and back into the woods towards the tunnel entrance. After fumbling for the correct key we entered the tunnel and raced back towards the cabin. I wasn't sure we were going to be in any shape to help Mack when we got there, I was breathing so hard I thought my heart was going to jump out of my chest at any minute. When we reached the big room below the closet Mark said, "I will go first, you back me up."

Rushing through the door of the closet, Mark rushed into the cabin and called to Mack. Mack and Jim came around the corner together. As I came out of the closet Mark was reaching for his pistol. I said, "Mark wait."

Mack asked, "What is going on, you both look like you have been scared by a ghost?"

I said, "Jim did you come into the cabin alone?"

Jim replied, "No, I came into the cabin with Robert Jennings. He works for the New York agency, I told you about him. He has something to talk over with us."

Uncertain who to trust, I said, "It looks like I am going to have to ask each of you to place your weapons at my disposal one more time."

Mack complied with my wishes immediately; again Jim was slow to agree. He did however place his weapon on the floor, as did Robert. When I felt as though we had the advantage I invited everyone to come into the kitchen and sit at the table. I said, "Make sure to keep your hands above the table at all times until we can sort through this whole mess."

Jim began, "This is Robert Jennings, I told you about him working with me in New York."

Mark interrupted, "Jim please hold your explanation until we determine what Mr. Jennings is doing here and how he knew where we were."

Jim started to reply and Mark interrupted again, "Jim, I don't want you to talk again unless we ask you a direct question."

Mark turned to Jennings and said, "Who told you where we were and why are you here?"

Jennings replied, "Jim told me where you were and the President asked me to come here."

I said, "When did Jim contact you?"

Before the question could be answered Bill came hurrying down the hallway. Half out of breath he said, "Mark come and help me pick up these pistols."

Mark jumped from the table and went and helped retrieve Mack, Jim and Jennings' pistols. Bill then entered the room and announced, "If you plan on living until tomorrow you better follow me."

Without a word everyone followed Bill down the hallway, I made sure that I was behind everyone else. As we entered the closet I called to Mark and said, "Mark, watch them until I get to the stairs."

Mark replied, "Not a problem."

When everyone was through the closet I pulled the door shut and sealed the false wall from the inside. At the bottom of the stairs Bill was waiting on everyone. When we reached the landing he said, "I am not sure who tipped the government where we were but there are about three teams outside and I don't think they are amateurs."

I looked at Jim and said, "You have about thirty seconds to explain why you would breech security and allow this joker to bring these teams in on us."

Jim said, "I was ordered by the President to make sure we linked up with Robert before you were allowed to enter D.C. The President wanted to make sure you were able to complete your mission and didn't feel as though you could be trusted to survive what Paul Warren was capable of throwing your way."

Suddenly the cabin was under fire. Bill reached for the lever at the escape tunnel and said, "If you plan on coming with me you better hit the tunnel."

The smoke from the tear gas began to seep under the door at the top of the stairs. There was a full-scale invasion-taking place inside Bill's cabin. I replied, "Without our cases we won't have the tools we need to get the job done properly."

Bill laughed as he shuffled his feet and moved deeper into the tunnel. He then replied, "If you mean the cases I have stored in the tunnel for you that were in the back of your truck, then perhaps I increased your chances of surviving, but not if you don't make it into the tunnel."

Entering the tunnel there were our briefcases just as Bill had said. Unsure who could be trusted and who could not be trusted I said, "Mark grab two of the cases and I will get the other two."

Mark did as he was asked and I grabbed the remaining two cases and moved deeper into the tunnel. Bill said, "Do you think they are in the cabin yet?"

I replied, "If they are following procedure thirty seconds after the tear gas was released they should be performing a full scale search and assault of the cabin."

Bill replied, "Then I guess now would be a good time for me to remind our guest that they weren't invited."

Bill pressed the remote detonator and the series of explosions shock the tunnel. We began to work our way through the tunnel; about mid way through the tunnel Bill surprised Mark and I by showing us an alternate tunnel that ran back towards the parking lot for the lake. We followed the light from Bill's flashlight. As he neared the end of the tunnel he leaned against the wall and waited on the rest of the group to catch up. Somewhat out of breathe from the brisk walk through the tunnel Bill said, "Mark, you and Chris go ahead and do your thing. I will stay here and guard these knuckleheads."

At first I was hesitant to leave Bill with the responsibility of guarding three men so I asked, "How are you going to guard these three guys and be able to stop any additional agents from coming up behind you in the tunnel?"

Bill smiled and flashed light on his remote detonator and said, "Why do you think I am carrying this thing, to give my hand something to do?"

After hearing this I knew Bill was capable of handling any situation in the tunnel. Mark and I grabbed our cases and Bill handed the keys to Mark. We headed up the ladder to the door. We pushed the door open enough to survey the area and then exited the tunnel. As we were leaving Mark dropped the keys back down to Bill. There were three vehicles parked on the lane near where Bill's cabin had stood. No agents were in view. The cabin had collapsed in on itself as Bill had planned trapping or killing anyone that was inside or outside if they were near the blast zone. Mark had opened his case and was assembling a sniper rifle when he said, "Pull out your binoculars and scan the area, use infrared."

I reached into my case and pulled the binoculars, I began to scan the area for heat sources as did Mark with his riflescope. We swept the area around the cabin and the vehicles then began to sweep the trees. I was about to conclude we were clear when I heard the safety switch off on Mark's rifle. I glanced over in his direction and he was sighted in on the rear of one of the government vehicles. I looked again through my binoculars for any sign of movement or heat source and saw nothing. I asked, "What do you see?"

Mark replied, "I am not sure but at the bottom of the second vehicle I think I see the heat pattern of feet."

I focused in on the bottom of the vehicle and there was a faint outline of feet. Mark suggested, "Stay here and watch that area, I will try and get a better vantage point."

I replied, "It would be better to be able to question this agent than to just eliminate him. Remember there are three guys down there with your uncle that we need to sort out who can be trusted and who can't."

Mark nodded and moved into the woods. I continued to listen for Mark as he moved away from me without taking my eyes off of the back of the vehicle. Mark moved like a native American, not even a leaf rustled as he moved through the woods. When I felt I had given Mark enough time to get to a vantage point I began to work my way closer to the vehicles using the woods as cover. After several minutes I was in position to view the back of the second vehicle. There was someone leaning against the back of the vehicle, he appeared to be hiding, this was not the posture of an agent.

Moments later I saw his hands move over his head as though he was surrendering. I scanned the area behind him and could see Mark had moved around behind him and appeared to be calling him back towards him. Apparently Mark was going to use the woods as cover and bring him back to me. I watched as they began to move back into the woods and could see them frequently as they moved among the trees on their way back to where I was waiting.

As Mark and his captive moved near enough to make them out without the aid of the binoculars I lowered them to my chest and waited on Mark to approach. I chuckled when I saw the captive was a young park ranger. I asked, "What were you doing behind that vehicle, trying to get yourself killed?"

The young man replied with fear in his voice, "No sir, I just wanted to see what had exploded. I was just about to go call the police when your friend here pulled his gun on me. By the way you know it is a federal offence to pull a gun on a federal officer don't you."

Mark looked at the young man as though he was terrified with the revelation that pulling a gun on a federal official was a crime and then he said, "I guess I will have to kill you right now since I don't want to be charged with a federal offence."

Before the young man could respond to Mark's statement I said, "Careful Mark we may need this young man to help us. Why don't you take him down to Bill and make sure Bill is still doing all right? I will stay up here and monitor for additional movement."

Mark agreed and the young man and he moved away towards the tunnel entrance. I began to scan the area again attempting to identify any additional agents that might have survived the blast. After several minutes of scanning the area I moved back towards the tunnel. Upon entering the tunnel the environment was extremely hostile. Mark tried to defuse the situation before I got there but his people skills were less than adequate. When I reached the bottom of the stairs I demanded, "What is going on here?"

Jim said, "I think it is time that you decide who you can trust and who you can't."

Mark replied, "It should be obvious to you by now. We trust each other and Uncle Bill. Other than that we are pretty much up in the air."

Jim insisted, "After everything that I have done to keep you two alive and you still don't trust me."

I interrupted, "Jim, it is not that we don't appreciate everything you have done for the team. Look at this situation from our perspective. We have found that every time we start to trust you we are being disappointed by your poor decision making skills or by just not telling us the whole truth about things. Until we discuss why Jennings is here or who informed the agents where we were hiding out I don't feel we have much choice but to keep your weapons. I am sure if the shoe was on the other foot you would react the same way Mark and I are reacting."

Mack said, "I tend to agree with Mark and Chris, it is not up to them to decide who can be trusted and who can't when there life is on the line. At the same time I am offended that you made me surrender my weapon, after all I have done nothing to prove I wasn't trust worthy."

Again I interrupted, "Now is not the time to discuss who can be trusted, we need to get to a vehicle that will hold all of us and that is not marked before the FBI, police, or more agents arrive to investigate this whole incident. I don't want to risk getting back into my truck either."

Mark and I gathered the briefcases and Mark climbed the ladder out of the tunnel, followed by Bill and the others. I was the last one out of the tunnel and as I exited the tunnel Bill pressed the remote detonator to collapse the remaining part of the tunnel. The explosion shook the ground. Startled by Bill's actions I asked, "Why did you do that, don't you realize there could still be some agents around?"

Bill replied, "I did it because I planned to do it all along, and as far as realizing there could be agents around indeed I do. There could have been some that survived the first blast and were hiding in the tunnel or my work room, either case they aren't there now."

The young ranger spoke up and said, "I am not sure what you guys are into and I am sure it is none of my business but if you will let me go I have a suburban that you can take."

I replied, "If we let you go we will need at least an eight hour head start before you contact the authorities so we will have time to get to Canada."

Bill said, "I am not sure that trusting anyone right now is the right thing to do. It is going to be crowded inside the suburban with six adults, if the ranger tags along that will be seven. Of course we could kill him and stuff his body into the back that wouldn't take up much room."

I wasn't sure if Bill was joking or serious about killing the ranger but I knew I didn't need one additional person to watch. We had to figure out who we could trust but now was still not the time or the place to do that. I really didn't care if the ranger called us in immediately, the main thing was that he believed we were leaving in his suburban that would give us the time we needed to stash the vehicle and transfer into my truck. I called a mini conference with Bill and Mark to explain my plan. I said, "We have to make the ranger think that we plan on using his vehicle, in the mean time I will need one of you guys to follow behind the rest of us in my pickup without the ranger spotting you drive off."

Bill replied, "I would rather follow you in the pickup than wet nurse those young pups you have with you."

Mark said, "Then it is agreed that we will let Bill follow us in the truck. Now how do we keep the ranger from knowing we are taking the pickup?"

Bill replied, "That hill over there is about a half a mile away. If you tell him he has ten minutes to get over that hill and out of sight before you shoot him, then I believe he will be more concerned with saving his own life then he would be watching our vehicle selection. I recommend you get the keys to the suburban first."

Bill's plan made since so that was what we did. Everyone except Bill loaded up in the suburban. Mark drove and I had Mack sit in the front seat, I got into the back with Jim and Jennings. We had just reached the main road when the sounds of sirens were heard coming up the road from town. I knew they were on their way to the cabin to investigate so I wasn't too concerned with them as we drove away in the opposite direction from town.

Approximately twenty miles from the lake we found a dirt road and pulled onto it. We followed it for about five miles. At the edge of some heavily wooded area I told Mark to find a place to drive into the woods. Several minutes later we were completely shielded from the air by a canopy of trees. This was a good place to find out about Jennings and determine who could be trusted. I had everyone get out of the suburban. Bill pulled the pickup into the woods and I asked him to load our cases back into the pickup. I was concerned now because

instead of our usual team of four we would be traveling with five or six people. Looking in Jennings direction I said, "Now would be a good time to convince us why we shouldn't shoot you and leave you here."

Jennings face grew red with anger and he said, "I am not sure what type of operation you think you are running but it was obvious to the President that you weren't capable of completing your mission without me. Now that I am here I keep asking myself why I bothered to try and bale you guys out of the situation back at the cabin."

Mark snapped, "Jennings there is only one reason you are still alive and that is because Chris hasn't asked me to eliminate you yet. As far as saving anyone, best I remember you were the one being led to safety by my uncle, not the other way around. If you knew the agents were coming why didn't you let us know that as soon as you arrived?"

Jennings replied, "When I reached the cabin I told Jim immediately about the agents coming and we were waiting on you to show up so we could leave."

I said, "That brings up another question, how you knew where we were in the first place?"

Jennings replied, "I spoke last night with Jim and he gave me directions."

"Jim? How did you speak with Jennings if I had the cell phone with me?"

Jim answered, "I called him on my cell phone."

"I assume you purchased a phone that is disposable."

Jim replied, "No it is my personal phone."

"Then you led the agents to us. I thought I explained all of this to you when we first met. We are not leaving a paper trail, do you remember any of that conversation."

Jim replied, "I was told to by Mr. Clarkston to stay in touch. I have only called him three times total. You can be happy that I called him this time or we would not have hooked up with Jennings."

I replied, "One of the times you called Mr. Clarkston was when we were in Salina, Kansas."

Jim looked shocked and said, "That is right, how did you know?"

Without responding to Jim's inquiry I said, "You also said I could be happy that Jennings is here. You were mistaken. I am not happy that Jennings is here; we don't need any more people to keep an eye on. I don't feel Jennings will be an asset to this team; all he has done by showing up so far is cast dispersions on Mack and you. The only good thing that I am glad about in this talk is that now I don't feel as though I need to watch Mack any longer. Apparently the talk we had the last time about half-truths and honesty didn't soak in. I refuse to take any more chances with you. I will leave you and Jennings here with the suburban and the rest of us will continue with our mission."

Jim snapped back, "No, I don't think that is what you are going to do. What you are going to do is follow my orders from here on out and we will do things the way I say. It was Mr. Clarkston's wishes that you be made to feel you were in charge, but the truth is, I have been calling the shots all along. If you thought you were going to do something different than the ultimate plan you are sadly mistaken."

Mark interrupted, "I never have taken a liking to you I always thought you were a weasel, but I guarantee you will not be giving me orders. I came along because Chris asked me to and nothing you could say will cause me to follow you."

Jim said, "Then you can stay here with the suburban."

Bill came walking up as though no one was talking and said, "The suburban has been wiped clean, all the equipment is in the pickup and it is time to go. If any agents are tracking the suburban they will be here shortly. I suggest the rest of this be settled further down the road."

Bill's advice rang with common sense. I said, "Let's go, we will finish this discussion later, but for now Mack you drive, Bill and Mark front seat, I will get in the back with Jim and Jennings."

Mack started the truck and I tapped him on the shoulder and handed him back his pistol. He didn't even acknowledge the jester, he simply took his pistol and holstered it and continued to drive. Still unsure what to do about Jim and Jennings I tried to think the events of the entire mission over in my head. I knew the most important thing that had to be done was complete the mission. It was no longer about the money, now it had become personal. If the President actually sent Jennings here to assist, I was determined to show him that I never fail to complete an assignment.

No one in the truck was talking, it was a very tense time when finally Mark said, "Chris if it makes sense to you I think we should down size this team. I propose Bill takes Jim's place and Jennings and Jim can be dropped off on the side of the road. If they won't follow directions then we can't trust them to be a team member."

I remained silent waiting on Jim to speak up and defend his position. After several minutes more of awkward silence Jennings finally says, "I have no intention of being put out on the side of the highway. I am an experienced agent and don't believe it would be in the best interest of this team to attempt to take down Warren or Brown without knowing their setup. I know exactly where they are and where they will be at almost every minute of the day."

I replied, "All right you have my attention, you have five minutes to prove you will be an asset to this team."

Jennings took a deep breath and said, "I won't need five minutes, what I have to say will only take about forty five seconds. Warren caused my father his life and I have been waiting to eliminate him for the past ten years only the agency was using him to track down other rogue agents. The agency is through with him now, partially because of your operation and partly because they feel I have waited long enough. Brown will just be a bonus for the agency."

"So what do your personal problems have to do with this operation? We are not on a mission of vendetta; we are here to eliminate a threat to this country's security."

Jennings said, "Without me you will not be able to catch Warren with his guard down."

Mark replied, "We don't need an advantage to take that maggot out, all we need is an opportunity. He knows we are coming and he will know we have arrived and all that knowledge won't give him any advantage. We will complete our mission with or without your help."

Jennings decided to appeal to our greedy side, he said, "I do not want any of the bounty that is on Warren, I only want the satisfaction of taking him out."

Mark asked, "What bounty?"

Jennings answered, "The fifty thousand dollars that the agency has placed on his head. Don't tell me you didn't know about the bounty. Each agent you guys have taken out had a twenty-five thousand dollar bounty on their head."

Scanning the truck for everybody's reaction, I realized that only Jim didn't react to this information as a surprise. I asked, "Jim did you know about the bounty and just decided not to share the information?"

Jim replied, "It is standard practice for the agency to pay for assignments. I knew we would be paid for our efforts only I didn't know the actual amount until now."

Mack pulled the truck over to a roadside park, without a word he parked and got out and began to walk towards a picnic table. He perched on the top of the table and waited to see if we were going to join him. As we approached he said, "I admit that Jim staying in contact with Mr. Clarkston has jeopardized our operation, but in the long run it has helped us. We would not have been able to round up the rouge agents any easier than what happened back at the cabin. As far as trusting Jim, I don't have a problem believing he has our best interest at heart. So let's get past all this finger pointing and threats of leaving someone behind and decide how the six of us are going to ensure the final success of this operation."

These were more consecutive words than I had ever heard Mack speak. He was very pointed on his opinion and very direct. I said, "Don't hold back Mack let us know how you really feel."

The group began to laugh and I thought things could get back to some sort of normality when Bill spoke up. "You are going to listen to what this guy says because he is vouching for Jim. Who here can vouch for Mack? I never trust anyone that goes to great links to redirect your thinking anytime he feels threatened. Remember the silent type can't be trusted just because they are silent, they are the ones that try to blend in so that they will not be discovered."

There was some merit to the words that Bill had spoken. I myself had doubted these two guys several times during this mission, but never with just cause. Mark said, "Let's split into two teams of three. Since Uncle Bill doesn't trust Mack or Jim let's put him with them and since we don't know Jennings we will take him with us. Does anyone object to this plan?"

No one spoke up to agree with Mark or disagree with him. All I could think about was how many vehicles this was going to make that I have had to purchase during this mission. I knew in order to ensure that we weren't being tracked that new vehicles were necessary.

Finally I said, "Let's head to a dealership. If we are going to be in two teams then we will need two vehicles. Before we do anything else, I want any communication devices you might have."

Jim was hesitant to surrender his cellular phone but did so without a word. Mack asked, "Do you want the head sets from our cases?"

I replied, "Only if they are not still in your cases."

MANHATTAN SHOOTING

I waited for a response, when there wasn't anything else said. I exclaimed, "Let's get that new vehicle!"

At the dealership everyone stayed in the vehicle expect for Bill, I guess he thought he could help make a better deal. I scanned the used car lot for appropriate vehicles and found one GMC pickup that met my needs. Bill asked, "Do you plan on making me ride in the back seat of that truck?"

I responded, "No Bill, you can sit in the front seat or stay here, it doesn't matter to me. I plan on purchasing this truck and I don't plan on purchasing any additional vehicles until this mission is complete. Then I plan on back tracking to all the places I have abandon my other vehicles and retrieve them and re-sell them as well."

Bill looked a little angry about my lack of concern over his feelings but I was not in a popularity contest. I had a mission to complete and was uncomfortable with all the additional team members despite the circumstances, which drew us together. I have grown weary of the hunt and am ready for the payoff. I worked out a deal with the auto dealership and before long we were driving out with our new vehicle.

I sent Jim and Mack over to the new truck with Bill and waited until they were loaded then said to Mark, "Let's hit the road, we have already wasted more time than I planned."

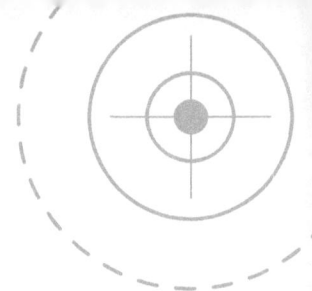

CHAPTER 26

ARRIVING AT D.C

We pulled into Washington D.C. around four thirty in the afternoon. We had been driving all day and I knew everyone must be tired. Mark said, "Let's take out Brown and Warren without the rest of the team. Jennings you said you knew where they were at all hours of the night or day. Why don't you make good on your statement and tell us where they are at?"

Jennings replied, "I will tell you where Warren is but not until you assure me I can be there when he is taken out."

Without discussing with me Mark said, "Not a problem. The only thing I want you to remember is if anything goes wrong I will hold you responsible and it is your life that is on the line."

Jennings answered, "I can be trusted, and I told you why I was here."

I decided this would be the perfect time to get Jim's story about the shooter confirmed. I asked, "Up at the cabin, was that the first time you had ever seen me?"

Jennings hesitated before he answered, "No, the first time I ever saw you was in Manhattan when Jim and I took out the agent that was assigned to assonate you."

I replied, "What did you do after that, please tell me everything?"

Jennings sat silent for a moment and said, "We turned Edwards over to the FBI and I returned to the shooters room and tried to survey your apartment the infrared binoculars to see if you were still alive. When I couldn't get a reading from the binoculars, Jim and I decided to check out your apartment. We crossed over to your building and went into your room, looked around for any signs of blood or a body. When we didn't see any evidence of injury we headed back down to the lobby. In the lobby we saw you talking to the police. We watched as you were escorted off. We followed you to the police station and then again when you went to pick up your pictures at the photo shop. We decided that was the right time to contact you but you got into a cab and drove to the Times building before we could speak with you. When you reached the newspaper office, Jim suggested I get some rest and he said he would stay in touch. That was the last I heard from Jim until a few days ago when he contacted me and said you could use some help completing the mission."

I replied, "If this is true, why didn't Mr. Clarkston level with me when I reviewed the pictures in his office? He knew you and Jim were the two men I mistook for police officers. Why didn't he say something then?"

Jennings answered, "Clarkston didn't expose Jim and I because he was ordered to keep our identity a secret. He did however give you ample opportunity to make the discovery on your own."

"By not telling me that Jim was a part of this mess he almost got Jim killed. Mark and I discovered Jim in the photos and Mark wanted to take Jim out with no questions asked."

Jennings said, "That would have been unfortunate but I don't think the government would have held you responsible."

"Being held responsible was never my concern, killing an innocent man would have been hard to live with."

Jennings replied, "The agency knew you were a good operative and felt as though the risks were minimal of you discovering Jim, therefore you were not informed. That way they could have someone on the inside reporting on your progress and making sure you didn't fail with your mission."

"Amazing, the agency wanted to ensure my success! Where were they for the other seventy or eighty missions I have accepted? I don't remember anyone assigned to protect me then and ensure my success."

Jennings appeared to be growing tired of answering my questions. He looked away for a few seconds before replying, "This mission was the most important mission you were ever assigned. With the homeland security act in place we were unable to track all the team members without the suspension of congress. If congress were to learn of the agencies covert operations on U.S. soil they would want to question everything we were doing and the bleeding hearts would come out of the wood work crying for due process of the law. This would allow many of the rogue agents to go underground or even leave the country. Once they were out of the country there would be no way to ensure their operations were shut down."

"So I was used by our government as bait, not as an operative. This whole thing about putting the pictures I took in the newspaper and paying me for the story was just a way to get me involved as a target to get my old group to come after me and expose them to the agency so they could be eliminated?"

Jennings appeared to be uncomfortable answering all my questions. I believe he knew the more I understood the mission the less suspicious I would be towards him. Jennings answered, "I guess that is close to the truth. The agency knew your background and was aware of your ability to survive. They were a little concerned that you are nearing the age that your awareness or edge if you will has dwindled. As for the money question the answer is yes. It was worth two hundred and fifty thousand dollars to the agency to get all the agents identified and hopefully eliminated."

Mark interrupted the conversation and asked, "Who was going to take Chris out if the mission failed or if he was going to be captured?"

Silence filled the inside of the truck. I had not given that angle any thought. It makes sense though that the agency would not want me to be captured once I knew about Jim, Mack and Clarkston. Jennings voice in a low near whisper said, "Mack. Mack was assigned to make sure you were going to complete your mission or die trying. If it is any consolation to you, Mack did decline the orders to eliminate you if the agents at the cabin had not been silenced. I think the kid has been taken in by you."

Distressed by the news I guess my mind shut down for a while, by the time I realized what was taking place we were pulling into position to observe a restaurant where Jennings believed Warren would be this evening. Bill, Jim and Mack parked back from us and on the opposite side of the street. When they realized we weren't going into the restaurant for supper they sent Mack over to question us. Mack said, "Why are we just sitting here? Are we going to eat or not?"

I replied, "Yes we are going to eat, but not here. Why don't you, Jim and Bill go find us something and bring it back? In the mean time we will wait here for you."

Mack seemed openly upset at my response but I didn't have the luxury of explaining the stake out to him. He stormed back across the street, slammed the driver's door to the vehicle and sped away. About forty-five minutes had passed when the came pulling in behind us. Jim got out of the truck and brought a couple of sacks with him. They had stopped and ordered us chicken fried sandwiches and fries. I opened the door to allow Jim to slip into the back seat. He too seemed irritated at my recent personality swing. I knew I owed him and Mack both a lot more than I could ever repay but I was not going to allow my personal feelings to dictate my opportunity for success. This mission had to be completed and it had to be completed by people I could trust, right now only Mark and Bill were on that list and the only reason Bill was on the list was because I knew I could trust Mark with my life.

We finished eating and Jim finally spoke up, "Is there any chance that you will let us know what your plans are now that we are in D.C.?"

I replied, "Sure my plans have not changed, I intend to complete this mission and I intend to be alive when it is over. The only way I know how to guarantee my success is by excluding you and Mack."

I know these words didn't set well with Jim; I could see the anger swelling up in his face. He acted as though he was going to debate the issue with me for a second, but instead he exited the truck and headed back towards the other truck where Mack and Bill were waiting. They sat behind us for several minutes until finally they started the truck and began to drive off. I never worried about where they were going because I was sure I had made myself clear that I didn't need their help on this part of the mission.

We had been sitting watching the front of the same restaurant for about fifty more minutes after Jim and Mack had driven away when two black SUVs pulled up in front of the restaurant. Several men got out of the SUVs but I still hadn't seen Warren. Finally the back door on the curbside opened up and out stepped Warren. He appeared to be worried; he scanned both sides of the street before continuing into the restaurant. I was sure he knew we were going to be hunting him down soon. We had already decided that the restaurant was not the right place to take this scum out. Instead we were going to tail him to his residence or an isolated area before we made our move. Mark said, "I am glad we were able to eat before this clown showed up because I am afraid I would have lost my appetite."

I was preparing to respond when Jennings said, "What the heck are your uncle and those other two jokers trying to pull?"

Looking in the direction of Jennings stare I notice Mack, Jim and Bill heading up the sidewalk to the restaurant. I jumped from the pickup and headed in their direction. Just as they were about to enter the restaurant I said, "Stand down."

Jim sent a stare like daggers in my direction and said, "Not this time old man, we have decided that you like the excitement of tracking more than you like the idea of completing the mission."

For the first time I was truly angry, before I could control the words coming out of my mouth I said, "Stand down or die."

Before additional words could be spoken Bill's pistol found the short rib of Jim and he said, "I think Chris wants to handle this from here on out. So why don't we go check in with your boss at the news paper and see if he has another assignment for you?"

A brief nod in Bill's direction to acknowledge my appreciation for his assistance, I backed away from the situation in the direction of my pick up. Mack walked towards me and said, "I am still the best sniper on the team and I would like to help you complete this mission if you will let me."

"You can come along with us but I can't guarantee you a shot. We are waiting on the opportunity to catch Warren in a less populated area."

We had only returned to the truck for minutes when Warren and Brown exited the restaurant and headed for their vehicles. We waited until they had driven by us before we started the vehicle and followed them. Jennings said, "They are headed for The Hampton area. Warren lives in that area."

We backed off of their vehicles and followed far enough back that they wouldn't suspect we were following them. As their vehicles entered a gated house we stopped along the street outside the home. Jennings and Mack exited the vehicle with their briefcases and took up position along the gate. We waited on Jennings to signal he was in place to take the shot then Mark and I drove away.

The headline story in The Times the following morning read:

In an ironic twist to the shooting that occurred fifteen days ago, today the FBI apprehended the Manhattan shooter identified as Paul Warren outside his home in The Hampton's. After a brief gun battle Warren and one additional man identified as Larry Brown were killed. The FBI states they were monitoring the activities of Warren on unrelated issues when he failed to voluntarily surrender he was taken by force.

Mark, Bill and I decided it was time to report into the agency and pick up our checks. I made one quick stop into The Times to collect my check from them. Mack met me at the door grinning ear to ear and holding an envelope with my name on it. He said, "The boss asked that I meet you here to deliver this to you. Clarkston said it would be better for all concerned that you just collect your money and leave. He added a bonus check to pay you back for expenses and the trucks you had to buy along the way. He also said it has been an honor to have met you."

I reached for the envelope and when I had taken it from Mack he extended his hand and said, "It has been a pleasure working with you, I am sorry that I didn't have an opportunity to be honest with you from the start."

I shook his hand and replied, "Everything worked out for the best and it has been a pleasure knowing you."

I turned to walk out of the building when a hand gripped my shoulder.

As I turned it was Jim, without a word he reached out his hand to me.

We shook hands and he turned and walked away.

Exiting the building I heard the honk of a horn, looking in the direction of the noise I noticed Bill and Mark sitting in my truck. As I neared the truck Mark said, "Don't think you are going to just drive off and forget about us. We are refugees and don't plan on becoming wards of the city of New York. You owe us a ride home."

Relieved to finally begin a short vacation before resuming my new role as a US Marshall I replied, "I couldn't think of two better people to spend my vacation with then you guys."

Bill interrupted, "What vacation! All you have done for the past few weeks is drive around and admire the countryside and lounge around in my cabin."

Smiling as I entered the passenger side of the vehicle I said, "Bill, that was work, don't forget every since Mark and I reached the cabin we had to keep up with you."

As we drove out of New York City Mark glanced in the rearview and said, "It is a nice place to visit but I am glad we are finally on our way home."

Glancing back at the city for one last look I noticed a Black SUV had taken up a position about three cars back. What did I care, we were on vacation.

After reviewing the pictures from the police station and noticing that one of the pictures of the shooters apartment exhibits an image of a man in the wall mirror. After enhancing the image and discovering the person was Jim Stephens. Why was Jim at the shooters apartment? Was Jim the shooter? He saved my life, why would he do that if he were the shooter? Mark will be in favor of having Jim eliminated without giving Jim a chance to defend himself. What should I do?

Mark Dillingham
Michael Sloan AKA Chris Moore
Mark Collins
John Clarkston—editor
Jim Stephens
Mack Murphy
Robert Jennings

Paul Warren and Larry Brown

www.ingramcontent.com/pod-product-compliance
Lightning Source LLC
LaVergne TN
LVHW041944070526
838199LV00051BA/2898